2

PHYSICS CAN BE FATAL

by

Elissa D. Grodin

For information, email **Cozy Cat Press**, cozycatpress@aol.com or visit our website at: www.cozycatpress.com

COZY CAT
P R E S S

ISBN: 978-0-9848402-8-1
Printed in the United States of America

Cover design by Cecilia Rockwell
http://coversbycecilia.daportfolio.com

10 9 8 7 6 5 4 3 2 1

ACKNOWLEDGEMENTS

There are a few people I would like to thank. Aubrey Andersen read the earliest drafts of the manuscript, and offered invaluable notes and suggestions that helped focus the story in the right direction. Dennyse Gunts supplied her own bit of detective work, and pointed out inconsistencies in a later draft. Physicist Cindy Keeler, a Harvard postdoctoral researcher, provided helpful insight into the heart and mind of my protagonist (Thank-you, Professor Strominger, for putting her in touch with me). And finally, my editor, Patricia Rockwell, guided the manuscript to completion by analyzing the story with the keen observations of the best detective.

Chapter 1

Absorbed in thought, Edwina Goodman stood in her small office staring at a chalkboard covered with mathematical equations.   Professor Donald Gaylord hovered in the open doorway looking amused.

"Adding a dimension?" he chuckled flirtatiously.

Edwina turned her head to look at Donald. She held a piece of chalk in mid-air, waiting. Her other hand remained buried in the front pocket of her jeans. Her wavy, chin-length, ash-blond hair was tucked behind her ears. Lips pursed in concentration, Edwina's longish bangs fell onto clear, hazel eyes.

"What's up, Don?" she replied, regarding Donald evenly.

Edwina was by now well seasoned in Donald Gaylord's excessive use of charm.   Along with countless other students over the years, Edwina had developed a crush on the disarmingly handsome Professor Gaylord in her undergraduate days. For his part, Donald Gaylord made a hobby of flirting, and was very good at it. Donald was a married man, and as far as the grapevine had it, he remained faithful.

Eventually Edwina made the discovery that Donald's habitual practice of conferring compliments and endearments was nothing more than standard operating procedure. Edwina's crush was short-lived. Her father would have probably called Donald Gaylord a snake oil salesman.

"Helen asked me to stop by," Donald gushed. "Have you heard the news? Alan Sidebottom has agreed to come to Cushing for the semester – it's all very last minute! I'm picking him up at the airport on Friday. Helen wants to know if you'll organize a department cocktail reception for Friday evening? If you're not busy?"

"Sure thing, Don," Edwina said.

"Terrific. I'll email you a list of stuff to order from Blackwell's. They'll take care of the food and the booze. Make the thing for 7:00. Tell them it's for about fifty people, and put it on the college account. Thanks a million, kiddo. You're a doll, you know that?"

Edwina listened to the rapid metronome of Donald's expensive Italian shoes clicking down the marble hallway. She turned her attention back to the mass of equations on the board, and put Alan Sidebottom and the cocktail reception out of her mind for the moment. Pushing her bangs out of her eyes in a familiar gesture, she returned to the engaging intricacies of the mathematical model on the chalkboard.

Bishop Larkin, one of the Department's most gifted students and a particular favorite of Edwina, knocked at her door.

"Come in," Edwina said without looking up from the chalkboard.

"Dr. Goodman?" Bishop said.

"Hi, Bish, come on in. Have a seat."

The gangling young man with dark, curly hair and tender eyes sat down rather awkwardly, his long limbs dangling from the chair like a great spider.

"I think I might be having a breakdown or something," he said in true earnest. "Not a breakdown, exactly. More like a crisis of confidence, or a kind of—
"

Edwina regarded the young man sympathetically.

"Why don't you just tell me what's going on?" she said comfortingly.

"Yeah. Well. I'm not really sure," he said, looking at the floor. "I'm not sure I should even be doing physics. I mean, I know I'm good at it, and I like doing it, but my dad's the one who persuaded me. I was thinking about studying comparative religion, maybe even going into the clergy. Just because my dad is some sort of famous chess genius everyone assumes he's brilliant in general—even when it comes to deciding what his kids' futures should be. I don't know if I'm doing physics for him or for me, or if maybe I might be missing a higher calling."

Bishop Larkin continued staring at the floor. He was having a conversation with himself. Edwina grasped this, and did not wish to interrupt.

"I'd probably feel horrible if I dropped out of the program," he continued. "I'm sure I'd feel like I was letting down a lot of people. Most of all, my dad. Maybe I'd be letting myself down, too. I'm not sure. It just bugs me that my dad thinks of me as his 'report card to the world'—his prize brainiac, as if my sole purpose in life is to show everybody what a wonderful person he is—you know—reflected glory and all that."

Bishop fiddled with his shoelaces. Finally he looked up.

"What do you think, Dr. Goodman?"

"I don't know, Bish," Edwina said, pushing her bangs to the side. "I'm pretty sure a lot of parents encourage their kids in certain directions, and all parents want their kids to do well. I think that's in the parents' manual. Maybe nudging you toward studying physics was your dad's clumsy way of letting you know how highly he thinks of you. How proud of you he is. In any case, I wouldn't focus very much on that. Focus on yourself, independent of your dad." Edwina let her words sink in.

"And as far as physics goes," she continued, "speaking for myself, now—I enjoy spending my time thinking about nuclear particles that only exist for a billionth of a second," she grinned.

Bishop smiled.

Edwina pointed to a printout of a favorite quote she had framed and hung on the wall of her office.

Don't ask what the world needs. Ask what makes you come alive, and go do it. Because what the world needs is people who have come alive. ~ Howard Thurman

"You can't tell me doing physics doesn't make you come alive, Bish, because I've seen it time and again. I see it every time you're in the lab," Edwina chided. "I think physics can be sort of a spiritual thing for some people, maybe we're our own brand of clergy. Carl Sagan said a great thing about science being his informed version of worship. I think that's how I feel about it."

Bishop thought this over for a moment.

"I guess I do, too," he said.

"As for studying comparative religion," Edwina continued, "the funny thing about that is, those guys you like to read—Alan Watts and Joseph Campbell and company—those guys end up with the same conclusions physicists do. That everything in the universe is connected. That we humans are—what does Brian Cox say?—we humans are 'the cosmos made conscious and life is the means by which the universe understands itself."

Bishop stared at Edwina.

"Don't be too hasty about turning your back on this stuff, just because you've got some issues with your dad," she said. "Separate the two, your love of physics and your resentment toward your dad. Think of yourself as a physicist with father issues," she laughed. Bishop Larkin stayed for forty-five minutes longer, chatting and laughing with Edwina. By the time he left her office, he was feeling decidedly sanguine.

*

Edwina Goodman was one of those fortunate creatures who stumbled across her true nature and felt in concert with it at an early age. Luckier, still, was having parents who did not put obstacles in her path. Her Uncle Edward, after whom she was named, gave Edwina a compass on her eighth birthday. Once the notion of the magnetic North Pole was introduced, Edwina became obsessed with investigating the unseen forces that operate the universe. She was the only child of doting parents who encouraged her every endeavor, even dismantling household objects in order to observe their inner workings. The things Edwina did not understand excited her the most.

Sometimes teased at school for being a tomboy or for having her 'head in the clouds', Edwina took little notice. The tomboy criticism registered no negative meaning to young Edwina, since she scarcely knew what was meant by it. According to her view of things, if you couldn't climb trees, build forts, run like the wind, and catch turtles and frogs, what was the point of it all? As far as having her head in the clouds, Edwina assumed it was a state to which everyone aspired, since what better place to get a bird's eye view of the world than up in the clouds?

It's true she could, at times, seem preoccupied, but this was because her focus was often directed toward some problem related to the invisible workings of the physical universe in all its glorious connections. The difficulty in this way of seeing the world was that she had a habit of tuning people out. Edwina would simply stop listening at the drop of a hat, if an idea worth thinking about caught her fancy and demanded attention.

Edwina was a devotedly 'glass-half-full' sort of person, like her father. Nathan Goodman owned a small fabric store and had never missed a day of work. He derived satisfaction from his relationships with the regular customers, and took pleasure in catching up with all their news, year-in and year-out. When Edwina was little he would bring home a beautiful button from time to time—one with a fake pearl, or a sparkling piece of jet—Edwina considered them as precious jewels and kept them in a prized box along with her compass.

Edwina's positive outlook was as much in emulation of her father as it was in reaction to her mother, who became increasingly languid as Edwina got older. Sarah Goodman napped a good deal during Edwina's teenage years. She went through the motions of being a homemaker while in a state of detachment which neither Edwina nor Nathan could interpret. She gradually stopped sharing her thoughts and feelings, and Edwina grew tired of asking, eventually thinking of her mother as a *depressimist*, someone for whom not only had the glass of life become half-empty, it was chipped and dirty. But true to her nature, Edwina put her focus on other things, more engaging things.

"It took years for your mother to get pregnant," Nathan once confided to his daughter. "The doctor didn't know why, or why she couldn't get pregnant again. Finally, when you were born, she was so happy —we both were. She doted on you—do you remember? All those tea parties with your stuffed animals, and cupcakes your mother baked, and her best teapot filled with real Indian tea . . . and do you remember the campfires in the back yard on snow days home from school? Your mother would bundle you up and make a big thermos of hot chocolate, and the two of you would go on an expedition, roasting marshmallows and building a snow fort. Do you remember all that, Edwina?" Nathan asked.

"One time she sewed a little papoose out of a piece of blue dotted Swiss fabric I brought home, so you could carry your favorite stuffed animal with you—a bunny rabbit, I think it was?—you wanted to take him along when you and your mother packed picnic lunches and hiked in the woods along the creek in the summertime."

"Of course I remember," Edwina replied. "It was all great fun."

Nathan had a way of looking at Edwina when she knew he wasn't really seeing her at all. He was flipping through a photograph album in his mind's eye. Photos of Sarah and Edwina, when she was a little girl, when Sarah was happy. The years filled with the pleasurable commotion of child rearing.

"Any-hoo," Nathan sighed, staring off into the distance.

Crickets.

"I suppose she just didn't quite know what to do with herself," he continued after a long pause, "after you grew up, and there were no more children to look after. She so wanted more children. I tried to get her interested in this and that—helping out at the store; charity work with some of her women friends; classes at the college—things like that, but nothing stuck," he trailed off.

"Well," Edwina said, "we all had a lot of fun back then, Pops. A lot of fun. And maybe Mom will find something, yet. Maybe something working with little kids? Something to really interest her, and get her going again. I guess it's never too late."

Nathan slowly turned to look at his daughter.

"I guess not," he smiled ruefully, in a way that signaled they both knew this would likely never happen.

*

A few words about the inception of the Physics and Astronomy Department at Cushing College would perhaps not go amiss, in particular the story of Sanborn House's outlandishly extravagant founder.

Equal parts brilliant scholar and unregenerate scoundrel, Professor Theodore Asa Sanborn gifted part of his family fortune to the college in the early 1800s, for the construction of a building devoted solely to the study of physics and astronomy. Still considered one of the most beautiful buildings on the Cushing College campus, Professor Sanborn's stately late-Georgian structure sits on the central Green of Cushing's park-like two hundred acre campus.

A true polymath, Sanborn taught himself Chinese and Greek so he could read ancient philosophy. Exceedingly hands-on during the construction of Sanborn House, Professor Sanborn directed that his favorite quotation be painted in gold leaf over the mantle piece of the main fireplace in Sanborn House's library. It remains there to this day, and reads, *"A good traveler has no fixed plans and is not intent on arriving ~ Lao Tzu"*. As far as the western hemisphere's admiration and appreciation for eastern philosophy, Theodore Sanborn was ahead of his time.

Although he ended up in the history books more for his philandering exploits than his academic ones, Professor Sanborn was at the forefront of several exciting scientific breakthroughs of his day. He had been of great help and inspiration to Michael Faraday in his seminal work plotting magnetic fields, and had also assisted Charles Babbage in building his prototype calculating machine. Professor Sanborn's ultimate disappointment over failing to achieve the scientific fame he hoped for in his own right, was perhaps due to his overactive personal life. His private journals confirm that Sanborn had a string of dalliances, all with married women. Three such relationships resulted in court cases. On one occasion, shot in the arm by a jealous husband, Sanborn declined to bring charges against the man, but continued his romantic involvement with the woman in question. The poor husband went mad and was eventually institutionalized. Sanborn never married, but twelve offspring were documented.

Professor Sanborn bequeathed a voluminous collection of books and papers from his personal library to the new library at Sanborn House, including colorful correspondences with many women, notably Sarah Josepha Buell Hale, novelist and editor of *Ladies' Magazine and Literary Gazette*, whose brother attended Cushing College. These lively writings, which would make most readers blush, are endlessly footnoted in articles and books chronicling the roguish life of Theodore Sanborn.

To promote the new library, Sanborn innovated the tradition of afternoon tea. Weekdays from four to five o'clock tea and cakes were—and still are—served in the sumptuous surroundings of Sanborn House Library, where carved butternut paneling on the walls and ceiling, elaborate marble fireplaces, Oriental rugs, and overstuffed chairs continue to evoke the feeling of a private library in a country manor house. For generations students and teachers have been coming together to enjoy refreshment and conversation in this rarefied atmosphere.

But his oddest stroke of all was yet to come.

Professor Sanborn's final bequeath to the college was the entire remainder of his family fortune, with the proviso that he be present at all future meetings of the Physics and Astronomy Department. He had read about the English moral philosopher, Jeremy Bentham, having such an arrangement at University College London. In his will of 1832 Bentham left directions for his body to be preserved and sat upright in his usual writing position, enclosed in a case to be wheeled into future board meetings at the college. The display case came to be known as 'The Jeremy Bentham Cabinet'

Accordingly, Professor Sanborn's body is preserved in a mahogany and glass case mounted on wheels, where he sits with a cheerful expression in a silk-upholstered chair, dressed in his best suit of clothes. The task of wheeling Professor Sanborn out for all department meetings falls under the job description of the Sanborn House Librarian.

*

A life spent entwined in the hierarchy of academia, with its reputation for petty jealousies and even viciousness, can be ulcer-making. Years spent wondering if and when one will succeed in getting to the next higher rung—the pressure to publish or perish––these things can wreak all sorts of stress and tension, unleashing pent up hostilities. It takes a firm hand and a cool head to run a smooth department. Theodore Asa Sanborn would have been impressed—and possibly intimidated—by the leadership qualities Dr. Helen Mann possessed.

As Head of the Physics and Astronomy Department, Dr. Helen Mann was outspoken, intrepid and opinionated. Dr. Mann operated in a very different style from her predecessor, Professor Emeritus Martin Jacobson, a genteel, pipe-smoking, scholar, liked by all and feared by none. When he retired and appointed her the new Head, Helen Mann wasted no time instituting a more corporate approach to the business of academia. She kept a sharp eye on the bottom line, and made individual performance her business, taking it upon herself to coach her department on everything from teaching style to wardrobe, much to their unanimous consternation. No one could argue that Helen wasn't devoted to the Department, and that she didn't tirelessly advocate for its academic prominence, if not dominance, in the field. She could be overbearing at times, even polarizing people, and there was the occasional fall-out. Still, she did a good job of running an efficient department, and people generally knew where they stood with her. Six feet tall in stockings, Helen cast an imposing figure, indeed.

Helen was responsible for losing one of the Department's brightest stars, Marjorie Harbottle. Professor Harbottle, a brilliant astronomer with an international reputation, had left her position at Cushing during the previous year. She had come to this decision shortly after Helen called her in for a meeting.

"Marjorie," Helen began. "Life's just too damn short to beat around the bush. Let's talk about a makeover."

"I beg your pardon?" a stunned Professor Harbottle replied.

"Let's neither of us be coy, shall we? It's your weight, Marge. I can't have any of my faculty being the butt of jokes around campus, no pun intended."

"I didn't realize . . . "gasped Professor Harbottle.

"No need to dwell on this," Helen interrupted. "Let's see if we can't get you on a diet program with a goal to drop—say, thirty or forty pounds?—by springtime. You'll be speaking at commencement this year. A lot of alumni and other important folks in the audience. A lot of endowment money riding on it. What say we get you in the best shape of your life? And afterwards, I'll take you shopping for a whole, new wardrobe! And I've got the best personal shopper in the business!"

Professor Harbottle had secured a new position at Princeton within the academic year.

Helen's private life was a favorite topic of gossip and speculation around the department. Among many colorful scenarios one rumor had it that Helen fell deeply in love with one of her professors during graduate school, and when he broke it off, Helen swore off men. One version of this tale included a baby who either died or was adopted. Others speculated that Helen perpetuated this story as a subterfuge to protect the fact that she did not like men at all and never had. Helen's regular trips to Boston fueled this idea of a 'Boston marriage'. Another view was that Helen was asexual, that her satisfaction came from work and work alone, and that her preferred outlet for pleasure was shopping. Helen dressed impeccably and expensively, and accessorized to freakish perfection.

In her quest to promote the Physics and Astronomy Department, Helen sent out an invitation to an academic superstar from Cambridge University to teach at Cushing for the fall semester. Noted scholar and leading string theorist, familiar television personality, and best-selling author, Distinguished Professor Alan Sidebottom was well known to the scientific community and beyond. Delicious stories and rumors abounded of his eccentricities and escapades, indiscretions and scandals. Urban legend recorded that he once demolished a London bookshop display window when it featured books on scientology (there was method to his madness). Alan Sidebottom had earned his reputation as the bad boy of theoretical physics.

And so when Professor Sidebottom did not respond at first to Helen's invitation, she did not allow herself to feel the disappointment, but simply turned her mind to coming up with another idea for increasing The Department's standing on the international stage of theoretical physics. But then, at the last minute, Professor Alan Sidebottom changed his mind and decided to come to Cushing, after all. Helen was over the moon. She left Sanborn House early to go shopping.

Her colleague in the Department, Associate Professor Mitchell Fender, strolled jauntily into Sanborn House after lunch.

"Hello, Ruth!" he chirped to the Department secretary.

Mitchell Fender was well aware of Helen's invitation to Professor Sidebottom, but was under the impression that Professor Sidebottom had turned the invitation down. Helen had not yet shared the news that Professor Sidebottom would soon be arriving in New Guilford to join the Cushing College faculty for the semester. Mitchell had strong reasons for wanting Alan Sidebottom to keep as great a distance from Cushing College as possible, reasons to which the whole department was privy. Mitchell was about to have his bubble mercilessly burst by the announcement of Professor Sidebottom's plans to come to Cushing, after all.

Loquacious and garrulous to a fault, Mitchell Fender oozed with bonhomie, but lacked the self-discipline and serious mindedness necessary to climb the ivy ladder. Five feet, nine inches in height, Mitchell carried his considerable weight in front of him, and looked as if he were going to burst out of the suspenders he always wore. He sported a walrus moustache, and a curly fringe of gray hair encircled his large, shiny head. Underneath his intermittent commitment to scholarship and habitual long-windedness, Mitchell Fender was a lonely man.

"Wrap it up, Mitch," Helen interrupted Dr. Fender during a departmental meeting, tapping her watch while Mitchell made a ramblingly random observation about an irrelevant issue.

"This is strictly N.G.I. (Not of General Interest), kiddo. Let's not waste Professor Sanborn's time, shall we!" Helen barked at Mitchell Fender. Mitchell chuckled amiably, as if he were the teacher's pet, and Helen was singling him out for some good-natured ribbing.

Mitchell Fender had managed to publish only two articles by the age of sixty. It was this paucity of published work that had stymied his promotion to full professor. Mitchell was discovering that being a middle-aged associate professor—and unwitting department jester—could, at times, be frustrating. Still, he managed to maintain a jovial demeanor in and out of the classroom, as best he could. Even in the face of terrible disappointment.

The previous year Mitchell had made the astonishing allegation that seven years of research toward a book he was working on, were stolen out from under him by Alan Sidebottom. When Professor

Sidebottom published a best-selling book based on work Mitchell claimed to be his own, legal steps were taken but nothing was ever proven, and the matter fell by the wayside. This blow to Mitchell's career was made considerably worse when Mitchell's wife of thirty years abruptly left him.

Thus, Mitchell Fender felt vastly relieved when he thought Alan Sidebottom would not be coming to Cushing. Mitchell believed in his heart that the Distinguished Professor from Cambridge was the cause of all his troubles.

Chapter 2

Surrounded by a flotilla of crisp, paper shopping bags with brightly colored tissue paper exuberantly announcing purchases yet unpacked, Helen Mann sat on her bed at nine-thirty at night with a glass of claret by her side. Bent over a laptop, she sent an email around the Department, requesting that everyone attend a brief Department meeting at eight-thirty the following morning.

The next day, impeccably dressed in a charcoal wool suit and mint green silk blouse, Helen strode confidently into the conference room on the third floor of Sanborn House at 8:25. Ten minutes later everyone had arrived and were seated around the long conference table. They chatted and drank coffee out of paper cups, waiting for Helen to start the meeting.

"I'll make this brief," she addressed them. "I know some of you have nine o'clock classes, so I won't keep you long."

She gazed triumphantly around the table, and breathed deeply.

"I have an announcement to make," she said. "Perhaps the biggest coup of my tenure as Head of Department so far.

Helen bowed her well-coifed head, allowing a moment for the occasion to sink in. Faculty members rolled their eyes and stifled chuckles at the absurd pomp of it all. Helen looked up with the victorious expression of a successful self-promoter. Gone were the days of modesty. Sir Edmund Hillary had made less of a fuss at the press conference after he conquered Everest.

"Distinguished Professor Alan Sidebottom from Cambridge University will be joining us at Cushing this semester. It's a real feather in Cushing's cap!" she beamed.

"Hear, hear!" bellowed Mitchell Fender, leading the accolades. "Well done, Helen, very exciting news!" Everyone seated around the table knew Mitchell's enthusiasm was disingenuous. Only Helen Mann, preening with pleasure, took his laudatory words at face value.

"I thought you'd all be pleased," she purred with an expression of self-congratulations.

To Helen's great frustration, the mood among the faculty did not budge from low-key. The idea of a celebrity colleague did not seem like nearly as much-of-a-much to most of them as it did to Helen. If anything, it seemed like much ado—another one of Helen's public relations maneuvers for Cushing College.

Edwina, seated next to Donald Gaylord, noticed that his jaws were clenching and unclenching nervously. He had not spoken a word.

"We're all set for Friday," Edwina addressed everyone. "Cocktail reception at seven Friday evening in the library. I'm sure I'll be wearing the LBD you've all seen me in fifty times," she laughed.

"LBD?" Ravi Kapoor turned to Paolo Rossetti.

"Little Black Dress," said Lois Leiberman, a petite assistant professor of astronomy, sporting pink-tinted eyeglasses and a pixie haircut."

"Right. Good point, Edwina. Thank-you for bringing that up," said Helen. "Dress appropriately, people, let's try and put our best foot forward. Suitable cocktail attire, please."

Seth Dubin appeared flush with excitement.

"Which courses will Professor Sidebottom be teaching?" he asked.

"Strictly graduate level," Helen replied. "I'll be working on his schedule over the next couple of days. Anything else?" she asked, looking around the table.

The meeting soon broke up. Feeling cheated from the cascade of kudos she had hoped for, Helen hovered near the doorway in order to salvage any remaining accolades. It was clear to everyone they would not be able to leave the conference room without congratulating Helen, so one by one they muttered 'nice job, Helen' or 'great news, Helen' on their way out. Helen's oversized ego wished for more, but these modest expressions of appreciation would have to do.

Mitchell Fender, deeply aggrieved by Helen's announcement, was suddenly dealing with a mild stomachache. He scurried out of the meeting rather quickly.

*

The Physics & Astronomy Department was soon humming with the exciting news of Alan Sidebottom's imminent arrival. For the next few days, faculty members spent more time than usual congregating in the Department reception area, drinking coffee and talking about this new development.

Ruth Benjamin, the department secretary, looked up from her desk.

"What the heck is going on?" Ruth said to no one in particular.

"A bigwig from Cambridge is coming to Cushing, Ruth," Lois said. "A superstar egghead! The guy is a real character—he's got a show on television, three best-selling books, and I heard they're even making a movie about him."

"I wonder who they're going to get to play Professor Sidebottom's part?" astrophysicist Ravi Kapoor said in liltingly precise English, his dark eyes shining in his handsome, brown face "It would have to be a cross between Harry Dean Stanton and Boris Karloff!"

"But it's not just the fame," chimed in Paolo Rossetti in a strong Italian accent. "It is the infamy, also! The dubious honor of having the most colorful reputation in all of physics, no?" A lock of shiny umber hair fell forward onto Paolo's long, thin face. He pushed it back from his forehead. "I have heard from more than one person that Professor Sidebottom got the wife of one of his college professors pregnant. They ran away together to Morocco, until he got bored, and returned to England! *Che tipo!*"

"Did anybody else read the trashy biography that came out about him a few years ago?" Lois Lieberman asked, through a mouthful of doughnut.

"Guilty as charged!" laughed Pete Talbot, a first year instructor. "There was a preposterously steamy incident in an airport bathroom—but who knows if any of it's true?"

The atmosphere around Sanborn House was frothy and boisterous. The last minute announcement that such an eminent celebrity in the field as Alan Sidebottom would soon be among them, induced downright giddiness among students and staff. The excitement over his arrival continued through the rest of the week. Faculty members carried on these impromptu coffee klatches in the Department's reception area, enjoying too many cups of coffee and doughnuts, exchanging Sidebottom stories, wandering in and out of each other's offices, discussing his work, speculating what it would be like to work side by side. After all, Professor Alan Sidebottom was a legend.

*

When each autumn brought new faculty to the bewitching New England town of New Guilford, they arrived with hopes of ascending the academic ranks from adjunct to instructor to assistant professor to associate professor to full professor. The majority were dedicated educators and scholars who approached their academic ambitions with a devotion to their students, a reverence for their subjects, and a healthy respect for their colleagues. The Physics and Astronomy Department was full of such people.

But Dr. Donald Gaylord was not one of them. At thirty-nine years of age, he was the youngest member in the history of the Department to become a full, tenured professor. A well-respected university press had published his hugely successful book, *Mind Your P's and Q's: Philosophy In A Quantum Universe.* The publisher had sent him on an extensive European book tour. In Rome he replenished his already superb wardrobe. Donald was on the fast track to academic success. The fact that his sites were set on becoming the next Head of Department was no secret to anyone.

If the Department had a poster boy, it would be Donald Gaylord. Athletic, tanned, and lantern-jawed, reminiscent of a Roy Lichtenstein romance comic book hero, Donald was popular with students for his engaging charm and classroom theatrics. Exuberant and mesmerizing at an auditorium lectern, outside the classroom Donald could be aloof and secretive. He was less adored by his colleagues than he was by his students. The general feeling among staff was that Donald stayed up nights plotting strategies to take over the Department, like some kind of demented general in a non-existent war. His wife worked in Boston as a personal chef, and that is where she lived. With no children, their commuter marriage had Donald spending weekdays in New Guilford and weekends in Boston, leaving him with plenty of solitary evenings to think too much.

*

Dr. Seth Dubin closed the door to his office and called his wife.

Sheila Dubin was sitting in the sunny living room of their home in New Guilford, painting her toenails 'Outrageous Red'.

"Incredible news," Seth said. "Alan Sidebottom is coming to Cushing!"

"Who?" Sheila asked.

"You remember, Alan Sidebottom!" Seth said. "I used to talk about him all the time in grad school—he's the reason I studied physics!"

"Oh, right, I remember. What's he doing in New Guilford?"

"He's teaching at Cushing this semester! I can't believe I'll actually be working with him! This is s-so incredible!"

Sheila Dubin, in her forties, earthily attractive, stared admiringly at her glossy, red toenails. She reached over to set down the nail polish, and picked up a jar of shea butter moisturizer, which she lovingly massaged into her feet. When she had finished rubbing the stuff in, she could think of nothing else to do to pamper her feet, now that she had trimmed, filed, soaked, scrubbed, painted, buffed, moisturized and polished them to perfection.

She and Seth had met during college. Sheila found Seth's gentle and cerebral manner very appealing, and more importantly, malleable. A gifted physics student, Seth was destined for great things, and Sheila thought he would go far in academia. She would be able to maneuver their life together however, wherever she liked. Seth would have his pick of universities to teach at, and together they would climb the ranks of academic success. She imagined all the beautiful places they would travel when he gave lectures and attended conferences around the world.

Sheila gazed critically around the small living room of the modest, one-story home. She had imagined more glamorous digs when Seth got the appointment at a top school like Cushing. Circumstances being what they were, Sheila felt increasingly frustrated and disappointed. She was tired of what she perceived as Seth's dithering lack of ambition. He seemed to be satisfied with research and teaching, contented to be in the classroom with his students, or in the lab doing research. He had less and less time for Sheila, who expressed no interest in his work.

She had her sights set on Donald Gaylord, that handsome paragon of upward mobility and ambition. Sheila considered being separated from his wife made Donald fair game. In turn, Donald seemed happy enough to be the object of Sheila's flirtations, although he received her attentions passively, and did as little as possible to advance the relationship. Sheila did not conceal her attraction to him, and Donald didn't hide the fact that he was flattered by the attention.

Sheila's work as an illustrator of medical textbooks had faltered when, after thirty-five years in the field, her publisher went out of business. Sheila got free-lance work as she could, but it was sparse. One curious consequence of having more free time was that she had started watching forensic procedural programs on television in the daytime. She had developed an insatiable appetite for these crime stories. The more baffling the cause of death, the more arcane the method of demise, the happier Sheila was. Hers was an exacting knowledge of the workings of the human body, and she had developed the habit while watching these programs of making illustrations of the deaths under investigation. Sheila's drawings were ghoulishly precise, as any illustrator of medical textbooks should be.

In her early years in New Guilford Sheila had gone back to school to take classes in chemistry. An enlarged knowledge of chemistry improved her skill set as a medical illustrator, and she started to incorporate into her drawings the effects on major organs of toxic chemicals in things like food preservatives, beauty products, and pharmaceuticals. Her portfolio had expanded to include highly detailed illustrations of organs degraded by poisoning, by chronic drug and alcohol abuse, and the like. She had a vague idea about compiling it all into a book one day.

In her spare time Sheila had also turned her considerable focus toward fitness, almost obsessively some thought, and began working out at the gym three times a week and running on the other days. Her interests and hobbies fell into a more or less earthbound category; she left a life of the mind to others.

Sheila picked up a small mirror and scowled. She kept her body so toned and fit she might have been mistaken for a much younger woman, if it hadn't been for the telling grooves on her face. Grooves and creases caused by habitually feeling disgruntled, by frowning and scowling too much. She leapt up from the sofa and ran to the bathroom, where she furiously rubbed facial moisturizing cream on her cheeks and forehead.

That's better, she thought with vain satisfaction, feeling optimistic about the wonders of modern science.

Sheila was a determined sort of person. She had places to go. Although Donald Gaylord seemed receptive to her romantic overtures, and despite her best efforts, their relationship had not achieved a physical level. Sheila was flustered by these moments of opportunity that seemed to keep slipping away. She feared Donald was trifling with her, leading her on for no reason.

Not one to back away from a challenge, Sheila pressed on, arranging dinners and secret meetings for the two of them, and ceaselessly continuing her campaign of self-improvement until the day she could crack the nut of Donald Gaylord. It would be her finest hour!

Donald's favorite topic of conversation lately seemed to be Professor Alan Sidebottom, and specifically, the hindrance to Donald's career Professor Sidebottom posed. When Sheila pressed Donald for details, he would vaguely reference Sidebottom's antagonistic attitude toward him—some old resentment over something—and then change the subject. Because Sheila's worldview lacked subtlety, she really had no great need for details. She could plainly see that Donald was unsettled by the older professor's presence at Cushing, and that was reason enough for her to take an adversarial stance. Professor Sidebottom would become her sworn enemy, too. Anything to ally herself with Donald.

Sheila got up from the sofa and prowled around the house looking for other ways to improve herself, ways to make herself irresistible to Donald. The little wheels started to turn and she began to focus on the possibility of a new avenue toward winning over Donald's affections.

She sat at the computer and typed in 'Alan Sidebottom'

*

Helen Mann knocked on Mitchell Fender's office door. She heard a soft 'thud' and a muffled response that she took for 'come in'. She swept into his office.

Helen's knock had awoken him. Mitchell stood up quickly from the crumpled sofa and cleared his throat several times. Clearly embarrassed, he hurriedly tucked in his shirt and attempted to smooth out the wrinkles in it with a series of brisk hand swipes.

"I've not been sleeping very well at night," he said apologetically. "I lay down for a short rest and must have dozed off. Please, sit down."

Helen took a seat in a chair facing Mitchell. She hunched forward, her pants-suited legs apart, elbows resting on her thighs, hands clasped. She evoked the image of a coach gathering her thoughts for a heart-to-heart talk with a struggling player.

"You should be taking something at night to help you sleep, Mitch. Stop by the pharmacy on your way home and pick up a sleep aid, okay? But that's not what I came to see you about," Helen said.

"I'm concerned about you and Alan Sidebottom," she continued. "We can't have any internecine feuds going on. Getting Alan here at Cushing this semester is going to translate into big contributions from our alums—and in turn, extra-funding for the department. I wouldn't blame you for whatever ill will you might harbor against Alan—everyone knows the man's a prick. Highly successful, but a prick, all the same. I just don't want the department getting sidetracked by having to choose sides in an old fight. I think you read me, am I right, Mitch? You follow me? We on the same page?"

Mitchell tapped the side of his nose with a forefinger.

"You can count on me," he said solemnly. "I'm a team player all the way."

*

Edwina arrived at Sanborn House early Friday evening. She knew her early arrival was not really necessary because of the fact that Charlotte Cadell, the Sanborn House Librarian, was nothing if not efficient, and lived for events such as these. Charlotte would have everything ship-shape for the reception, Edwina knew. But the job of organizing the cocktail party for Professor Sidebottom had fallen to Edwina in the first instance, and with a mostly unforgiving conscience, Edwina knew it was only right she be there early alongside Charlotte to make sure everything was as it should be.

Charlotte Cadell felt a deep devotion to the library, and indeed to all of Sanborn House. She had what could be described as an ardent attachment to the place. At forty years of age, the Sanborn House Librarian appeared more middle-aged than youthful. In part this was because although Charlotte was quietly pretty in a faded sort of way, she did not make much of a fuss about her appearance. But it was more than that. Charlotte had suffered a profound disappointment in her youth. Instead of moving away from this heartbreaking experience, she chose to remain attached to it. She allowed it to define her life. She measured all experiences before and after by this event. And after so many years of holding the disappointment close to her, it became the thing that comforted her. It was what gave her life meaning, and she allied herself fervently to this defining event from her youth. With no family of her own to look after, and none to look after her, Charlotte took her responsibilities at Sanborn House and in particular to the library, very much to heart   It was her province, her arena, her life.

Edwina, on the other hand, was girlishly lissome and people often took her for younger than her twenty-five years. With a spirited disposition circumscribed by indomitable curiosity Edwina gave the impression that somehow the downward pull of gravity had less effect on her than on other people, as if she weren't wholly earthbound.

Edwina was dressed in a short, black gabardine dress that showed off her slender figure. This dress came out of the closet anytime there was a 'do' at the library; it was her workhorse dress. Otherwise, her only concessions to the evening's function were a bit of mascara and a dab of pink lipstick.

Charlotte Cadell was busy fussing around the library, plumping sofa cushions and straightening tablecloths. Pressed white linens covered the long study tables. Glasses of champagne in perfect rows, and trays of nibbles sat at the ready, alongside damask cocktail napkins. The library was gleaming, and everything looked perfect.

"You look nice tonight, Charlotte," Edwina said, taking a glass of champagne for herself and handing one to Charlotte.

"Oh, thank-you, Edwina, " Charlotte said, brushing an invisible piece of lint from the bodice of her frock. "So do you," she added demurely.

"What do you think about our celebrity visitor?" Edwina asked.

Charlotte took a sip of champagne.

"Pretty exciting, I guess," she replied primly. "I'm not sure what to think—Professor Sidebottom seems to have quite a reputation. From what I've heard."

Edwina had the impression that Charlotte was parsing her words carefully.

"Well, all I can say is, I bet we don't have a dull moment around here all semester! Bottoms up!" Edwina said.

How true that would be.

*

The library filled up quickly. It looked as if the whole department had shown up. Teachers and students, used to seeing each other in the casual, everyday dress of jeans and fleeces, were turned out in various versions of cocktail garb, from patterned maxi dresses to suits and ties. Soon enough a convivial hum of conversation and laughter filled Sanborn House. The partygoers drank and chatted excitedly in anticipation of Professor Sidebottom's arrival.

Lois Leiberman stood in a group with colleagues Ravi Kapoor, Paolo Rossetti, and Seth Dubin and his wife. Paolo's umber hair was brushed neatly in place, and fell just over the back of his shirt collar. Like Ravi, Paolo wore a jacket and tie and jeans.

"You look fetching this evening," Paolo remarked, taking in Lois's ensemble of a chiffon skirt, black angora sweater, and black tights.

"This reminds me of my parents' cocktail parties when I was a kid," Lois said. "I remember sneaking downstairs to spy on them, and being shocked by the parallel universe in the living room. A sea of beautiful, glamorous people—the women in little black dresses and pearls, gossiping and smoking cigarettes—the men in suits and ties, looking very alpha and predatory . . .

everyone throwing back high balls like there was no tomorrow . . ."

"Seth, have a drink, for Christ sake," Sheila Dubin snapped. "You'd think it was your prom night and your date didn't show up, you look absolutely miserable."

Ravi Kapoor took a glass of champagne from a tray, and handed it to Seth. Ravi and Paolo clinked glasses with Seth.

"Cheers, my friend!" Ravi said, his dark eyes sparkling, as he patted Seth gently on the back.

"*Cin cin!*" said Paolo. "Drink up!"

*

A rangy six feet four, dressed in tweed jacket, corduroy trousers, and a pair of fisherman's sandals with thick socks, a wild mane of silver hair framing a bemused face, a blithely cheerful Alan Sidebottom appeared in the doorway of Sanborn House Library at eight o'clock, propped up by Donald Gaylord. Registering annoyance, but looking resplendent in an Armani suit, Donald settled the guest of honor onto the nearest sofa.

Professor Sidebottom promptly embarked on a loud conversation with anybody who happened to be nearby, and launched into an off-color joke about two string-theorists and a sausage, oblivious to the looks of consternation and astonishment around him.

Donald Gaylord sidled up to Edwina and slid his arm around her waist. His cologne smelled of orange blossom and amber.

"Sidebottom is smashed out of his skull!" Donald whispered in her ear. "He insisted on stopping for a drink on the way from the airport, and I couldn't get him back in the car until he'd had three scotches!"

Professor Alan Sidebottom looked distinctly relaxed. His rangy figure was comically folded into the deep-cushions of the sofa, his long legs crossed, a plate of hors d'oeuvres balanced precariously on one bony knee. He was gesturing broadly in an animated conversation until—inevitably—the plate of food fell to the floor.

"Goddamned Isaac Newton!" he laughed uproariously.

"He seems to be having a good time," Edwina said, observing all of this. "Why don't you just enjoy the party? Have a drink, Donald."

"Yeah, you're right. Nothing I can do about it," Donald said, straightening his tie. "Listen, would you mind very much seeing Professor Sidebottom home after the party? I can only stay tonight for an hour— I've got to get back to Boston. He's staying at the carriage house—it's only a five-minute walk. I dropped his bags off on the way here, and left the front door unlocked."

"Sure thing, Don," Edwina said.

Donald smoothed back his hair, picked up a bottle of champagne and roamed around the library like the lord of the manor—joining in conversations, dispensing compliments, and refilling empty glasses.

Mitchell Fender, to everyone's great surprise, chatted amiably with the guest of honor, his walrus moustache moving comically up and down as he spoke, his mouth concealed by it. Mitchell hooked his fat thumbs through his suspenders, and rocked gently back and forth on his heels as he traded stories with Alan Sidebottom, who was sprawled on the sofa.

Mitchell's colleagues were under the impression that since Mitchell had publicly accused Alan of plagiarizing his work, calling him out in a letter to the editor of *Reviews of Modern Physics* for theft of intellectual property, Mitchell would altogether refuse to speak to Alan – perhaps not even come to the party––let alone engage him in good-natured banter. But tonight Dr. Mitchell Fender and Professor Sidebottom chatted and drank companionably, making the whole, ugly thing look like a trifling spat.

"How many theoretical physicists specializing in general relativity does it take to change a light bulb?" Professor Sidebottom asked a blank-faced Mitchell Fender.

"Two!" a drunken Sidebottom shouted. "One to hold the light bulb and one to rotate the universe!"

Mitchell blinked his eyes solemnly like a Great Horned Owl, and suddenly doubled over, roaring with uncontrollable laughter.

 Edwina ventured across the crowded library carrying a plate of hors d'oeuvre and a glass of champagne for Professor Nedda Cake. Professor Cake, at eighty-nine years of age, the oldest member of the department, sat with two graduate students on a sofa in a quiet corner of the library. Professor Cake had shrunk with age from her youthful, willowy height, but was still a handsome woman with beautiful posture. Braided white hair encircled her head like a crown. She wore a heather gray sweater, a string of pearls and a dark skirt.

Edwina was glad to see her friends, Laura Brenner and Nate Harris keeping company with Professor Cake. She set down the food and champagne at Nedda's elbow, and joined the group.

"What do we think of our distinguished visitor?" Edwina asked.

Professor Cake took a sip of champagne, her eyes gleaming.

"I knew him when he was a student at Oxford, you know. Alan is a good scholar but he can be a rather disagreeable man," she said, biting into a date wrapped in crispy bacon, "when he's not busy being charming. Charm has always been the great English blight."

Professor Cake had the complete attention of Edwina and grad students Laura Brenner and Nate Harris. They were hoping she would elaborate on this tantalizing remark.

"Alan keeps rather a lot of secret arrows in his quiver," Professor Cake continued obliquely. "And he is quite ruthless about using them. Pick his brain, by all means, children, but keep your distance. Alan's moral compass broke a long time ago."

Nate Harris, a first year graduate student, was a wholesome-looking and bright young man. He reminded Edwina of Huck Finn.

"It took me a while to get through it, but his paper on dark matter completely blew me away," Nate said.

"Didn't he study with your husband, Professor Cake?" asked Laura Brenner, a second year graduate student.

"Indeed, he did. My husband taught Alan at Oxford before we came to the States. Alan was one of my husband's brightest—and laziest—students. He was a bit of a lad back then, and I doubt much has changed," the old professor chuckled, draining her champagne.

The moment of truth had arrived for Seth Dubin. Nervous as he felt, he was steeling himself to speak to Alan Sidebottom. Seth discreetly dried his sweaty hands and upper lip on a napkin, and approached Professor Sidebottom.

Unfortunately Seth's nerves got the upper hand, and an old nemesis showed up in the form of a childhood stammer. Seth hovered over Professor Sidebottom with his hand held out, unable to utter a sound. His lips were frozen around the formation of the letter 'p' for 'professor'.

Seth's wife, Sheila, instantly gleaned what was happening.

"Professor Sidebottom," she smiled warmly, reaching out her hand. "I'm Sheila Dubin. My husband, Seth, has been talking about nothing else but meeting you. And now, in all the excitement, the moment has rendered him speechless, I'm afraid."

Calmed by his wife's soothing voice, Seth was able to lower his outreached hand, but was still unable to speak.

"By god, a good, old-fashioned stammerer!" Alan roared. "Nothing for it but a good tug—stick out your tongue, man—don't be shy—I'll fix you up in no time with a firm yank!"

Mortified, Seth smiled weakly and shrugged. Sheila could hardly believe the thoughtlessness of what she had just heard. She stood frozen to the spot, her face darkening with humiliation and steely hatred for Alan Sidebottom's cruel treatment of her husband.

Helen Mann was on the other side of the library struggling with her own feelings of humiliation. She was straining under the acutely perceived insult of being ignored by the guest of honor. As the minutes ticked by and Professor Sidebottom failed to seek her out, thank her for the invitation to Cushing, and pay his respects, she grew increasingly affronted.

To cover her embarrassment at being publicly snubbed, she feverishly held forth to a small group of bewildered students about the possibility of the existence of ice inhabitants on the moons of Jupiter. The confused students snatched covert glances among themselves, tacitly agreeing not to say anything and not to move, until Helen's strange, verbal spasm was over.

Eventually Helen could bear Alan's rude and insulting behavior no longer, and—as she often did—resolved to take control of the situation. She strode across the room and made her way through Alan Sidebottom's growing coterie of admirers, carelessly pushing aside anyone in her way.

"Alan, dear boy!" Helen trilled, shoving Seth out of her path.

"*There* you are! You're going to *adore* staying in our little Carriage House! It's been written up in *Architectural Digest* you know, and *everyone* has stayed there over the years—Faraday, Maxwell, Einstein—."

Alan slowly gazed up at Helen, who was wearing a wrap-around dress of lavender faux-suede, and ropes of pearls around her sagging neck. A heavy application of make-up gave her face a slightly mask-like appearance.

"Will I be sharing a room with one of the lads, then?" Alan Sidebottom slurred, winking at the group of onlookers.

Good God, Helen thought, fuming, *he doesn't even remember me!*

*

The party sustained a pitched level of collegial conviviality for hours, more or less until the champagne ran out. When the library began to empty, Edwina introduced herself to Alan Sidebottom, and offered to escort him to the Carriage House. He stood up shakily. Fumbling for her hand, he lifted it unsteadily toward his mouth, finally managing a kiss, which turned into more of a lick.

"Edwina, you say? Not *Countess Edwina of Burma*, by chance?" The professor said with an engaging smile. "What a very pretty Edwina you are!"

"Did you enjoy the party, professor?" Edwina asked, gently steering him toward the door. Once outside, she guided him carefully down the front steps of Sanborn House.

"Indeed, I did. Absolutely delightful. "'Fraid I might have had too much to drink. I'll make my apologies tomorrow."

The night was mild and warm, more Indian summer than fall. The lighted path meandered through an alley of dense yew hedges, pruned to perfection over generations. Stars shone brightly in the black sky.

*

Helen Mann had slipped out of the party early and retreated upstairs to her office to regain her composure. From the darkened window she watched as Edwina accompanied an unsteady Alan Sidebottom along the path toward the Carriage House cottage. She watched as Professor Sidebottom suddenly stopped. In one remarkably awkward movement, he leaned down as if to embrace Edwina, tripped over his own foot, fell into the hedge, and threw up. For an encore he passed out.

Helen stood at the window. Tears ran down her face.

Oh, good Lord! Edwina thought. *I can't wait 'til I get to delegate these ridiculous tasks to underlings!!*

She has little idea what to do. Feeling for a pulse, Edwina was vastly relieved to find one. The carriage house was only twenty yards away, but she couldn't possibly carry him, and she didn't dare drag him along the ground. She fanned his face and lightly patted his face, repeating his name, but to no avail.

Two Cushing students came walking toward her along the campus path. Finding the situation at hand highly entertaining, the obliging students helped Edwina carry Professor Sidebottom the rest of the way to the Carriage House.

The cottage was unlocked, just as Donald Gaylord had said. Edwina and her cohorts lifted Professor Sidebottom onto the high, four-poster bed and covered him with a patchwork quilt. She expressed profuse gratitude to the students before they went on their way.

Edwina looked down at Alan Sidebottom's worn face. He looked peaceful, she thought. His was the face of a man who had engaged in a few too many dustups in his time, a face crisscrossed with battle lines. Edwina wondered how many of these fights he regretted. She wondered if he could remember what most of these skirmishes had even been about.

She looked around the quiet bedroom. A club chair and ottoman upholstered in striped silk suggested an inviting reading spot next to the windows. There was a dressing table in another corner with an old-fashioned three-paneled mirror on top, and a gathered chintz skirt that fell to the floor. A wicker, child's rocking chair sat next to the bedside table, its petite cushion covered in the same silk as the club chair. Edwina sat on the club chair ottoman, and watched Alan Sidebottom sleep until she was certain she could see his chest moving up and down.

On her way out of the Carriage House Edwina took a peek around. The other rooms were similarly appointed with comfortable, upholstered furniture and expensive antique pieces. A large, lidded porcelain tureen and a pair of silver candlesticks adorned the fruitwood dining table with twelve surrounding chairs. A rather grand English walnut desk dominated the study, where glass-front bookcases filled with leather bound volumes lined the walls. In the foyer a row of five nineteenth century portraits scowled down at Edwina with censorious expressions, castigating her for hanging around like such a curious cat.

"I'm going!" she laughed over her shoulder on the way out.

*

Mitchell Fender could not get to sleep that night after his usual bedtime bromide of hot milk and molasses. He reviewed his performance at the party as he tossed and turned in bed, getting the bedclothes into a miserable twist.

I was perfectly charming to Alan! Didn't let my real feelings show for a moment! I promised myself there was no way on God's green earth I was going to give him the satisfaction of seeing me upset, and by golly I pulled it off!

Mitchell looked at the clock. Three a.m. Exhausted, he sighed deeply and got up. After he finished re-making the bed, he sat on top of the covers.

No harm in another cup of hot milk, he thought, padding toward the kitchen in a well-worn pair of slippers his ex-wife had given him. Moonlight illuminated the kitchen, without need for the overhead light. Mitchell sat at the kitchen table, gazing out the window at the moonlight night, feeling comforted by the hot, sweet milk.

But how am I going to be able to pull off this act for the whole semester?

Resolve was not Mitchell's strong suit, but somehow he would come up with a plan. Suddenly he felt very tired and could barely keep his eyes open. He left the half-full cup of milk on the table and shuffled back to bed.

Chapter 3

Edwina lived in a small, rented house set on two acres of mostly overgrown land on Canaan Farm Road, ten minute's bike ride from campus. A typical Cape built solidly in the 1930s, the symmetrical little house had a white clapboard exterior, a centrally located front door and chimney, black-shuttered sash windows on either side of the front door, and two dormer windows above those. Edwina lived there alone, and felt very contented with the situation. Although economical, roommates were a vexed issue.

Kit McCrumb of the Baltimore McCrumbs was assigned to be Edwina's roommate their first year at Cushing. Kit was a shy, retiring girl who wore thick lenses in her glasses and had long, red hair, down to her waist. Edwina remembered thinking at the time that Kit's shyness might have been a protective response to her inability to see well.

Their dorm room had a pretty view of the river, and was spacious enough for two beds, two desks, two bookcases, two sizable closets. Kit's modesty dictated that she retreat into her closet and close the door every time she wanted to change clothes. Gradually she began spending more and more time in the closet, bringing in a lamp, a chair and her laptop to do homework, even setting up a folding cot for taking naps. Kit would only speak on the phone from inside her closet.

Edwina tried talking to her roommate about her shyness, and tried to engage Kit in social activities with some of the other students, like movies and shopping expeditions. But the shy girl rarely joined in these outings, and eventually started withdrawing to the closet whenever Edwina was in the room.

Edwina did not fare much better the following year, when her sophomore roommate was Sue Dillman.

Sue was a charming girl, lively and witty, with a figure like a twig. She kept a pitcher of bright red fruit punch on her dresser, which she refilled throughout the day as she guzzled the stuff—often instead of eating a meal. Just before Thanksgiving, the pitcher of fruit punch disappeared, and was replaced by a plastic storage box filled with candy and packages of cookies. Edwina wondered why Sue allowed herself to put on so much weight over the next few months, until one day when the plastic storage box disappeared and the fruit punch was back. Within a short period of time Sue was back to being a twig. And so it went, all year long, back and forth, with frequent late-night vomiting sessions in the bathroom. It was Edwina's introduction into the world of a bulimic.

The following year Edwina decided she had had enough of dormitory life. With a modest legacy from her Uncle Edward, Edwina scoured New Guilford for an affordable apartment, house, caretaker cottage, or cabin to rent, until she finally found her little house on Canaan Farm Road. Located on land that had once been part of Canaan Farm, the house was owned by an elderly woman named Essie Claxton, who had been born and raised at Canaan Farm, and who had inherited all the land and the old farmhouse and barn, which had fallen derelict from disuse. Essie Claxton now lived in a condominium in downtown New Guilford.

In the first year of her tenancy, Edwina discovered that the centrally located fireplace was not sufficient to heat the little house. Unable to afford oil heat, she purchased second hand a small, cast iron wood-burning stove for the kitchen, which heated the whole house nicely. Upstairs were two small bedrooms and a bathroom. Edwina had decorated the house with curtains she made herself from fabric picked out at her father's store, furniture collected at second-hand shops, which she re-painted in bright colors, and a few of her Uncle Edward's amateur watercolor paintings.

Her time at home was mostly spent working at her laptop at the long refectory table in the kitchen, piled high with books and papers. The kitchen was a light and airy room that had been re-configured before Edwina's time. Separating walls had been removed from a small dining room and adjacent vestibule, and these rooms had been incorporated into the kitchen, making it the nicest room in the house. A Dutch door communicated from the kitchen to the back yard, which was planted with maple and oak trees that kept the house cool in the summertime. Edwina had laid a small terrace in the back with slate pavers she salvaged—with Essie Claxton's permission—from the dilapidated barn at Canaan Farm. With no idea of how to do it properly, Edwina had used a hoe to scrape out an inch-deep footprint for the terrace, and then she laid the slate slabs together in a sort of patchwork. She purchased a little table and four chairs at the hardware store, and even though the terrace wasn't terribly stable, she enjoyed sitting out there.

*

Saturday was a beautiful fall morning, crisp and sunny. After breakfast Edwina washed the dishes, changed the sheets on her bed and threw in a load of laundry. Too nice a day to spend cleaning the house and grading papers, she put a few provisions into a backpack, jumped on her bike and headed toward the

Boat House on campus. Twenty minutes later she was launching her kayak into the water.

The river was wide and glistening. Edwina paddled slowly downriver, listening to the sound of her paddle hitting the water. She gazed at the trees along the riverbank, knowing they would look different the next time she paddled there, and still different the time after that. Chlorophyll production had halted for the year, signaling the trees to stop making food, and the lush summer leaves had mostly faded. The magnificent fall colors would soon arrive, turning the riverbank and countryside beyond into a landscape painting of improbable brilliance.

Edwina was on the lookout for a familiar outcropping of birch trees on the left side of the river. Once she spotted it, she headed the kayak toward the bank, and pivoted into a narrow passage that dead-ended in a little cove. She paddled toward the tiny shore, got out of the kayak in shallow water and pulled the boat onto the beach where it would not float away. Edwina had discovered the place during her junior year at Cushing.

She lay on the shore of this hidden bay, her eyes closed against the sunlight. Thinking about the events of the previous night made her feel weary, in particular the sad fact that Alan Sidebottom turned out to be a drunk, albeit a brilliant one.

What had Helen Mann been playing at? Edwina wondered. *She had been so rude to Seth Dubin, such a gentle soul—pushing him out of her way, like that— and then where had she disappeared to? Sheila Dubin was awfully upset—and good Lord, that dress she was wearing! Ridiculous, way too young for her . . . and what about Nedda Cake? What did she mean, hinting at Alan Sidebottom's dark side?*

The warmth of the sunshine was a tonic, a salve on these troubling thoughts. As Edwina lay on her back she visualized her toes, and traveling in her mind's eye slowly up her body, she pictured every single muscle giving way to relaxation, until all the tension in her body gradually melted away into the sandy dirt beneath her. All she could hear was the delectable sound of tiny waves lapping against the shore. She grinned.

Edwina opened her eyes. She watched the sparse cumulus clouds pinned against a saturated blue sky. Once again she let her mind wander. Her thoughts drifted beyond the blue sky to the blackness of space, to the planets and their moons—to Titan, Saturn's largest moon. She lazily considered the methane clouds at Titan's south pole and imagined the exotic weather patterns that might exist there. Quantifiable properties of things like stars and planets and galaxies were far more comforting to think about than the unruly mess of human relations.

*

Mitchell Fender sat at the cluttered desk in his cluttered office. He hung up the phone and stared out the window. Pulling a red bandana handkerchief from the back pocket of his trousers he blew his nose loudly, and continued staring out the window.

Gloria, you've done this to me! Mitchell thought angrily. *Leaving me after nearly thirty years wasn't enough – you had to will this thing to happen!*

He took a succession of shallow breaths until he was able to calm himself and breathe more deeply. He closed his eyes tightly.

Get a grip, Mitch. That's nonsense, and you know it. Simply nonsense. Man up, brother!

Mitchell Fender got up from his desk and grabbed the red, fleece jacket hanging on the back of the door.

"Fresh air's the thing!" he said on the way downstairs for a long, contemplative walk around campus before teatime.

*

"Why is tea so crowded today?" said Nate Harris, shoving a cookie in his mouth and gazing around Sanborn House Library. He dropped two coins into the payment basket.

"Probably because everyone's waiting to see if Sidebottom will show up, after his performance Friday night," said Laura Brenner, standing between Nate and Edwina in line at the tea table. "Do you have any more change, Nate? I don't have any money on me."

Nate dug into his jeans pocket and produced two more coins, which he flipped into the basket.

"Speak of the devil," Edwina muttered under her breath, picking up two gingersnaps.

Cups and saucers in hand the three settled onto a sofa next to the main fireplace. The library was, indeed, more crowded than it usually was at five minutes past four o'clock. On a typical afternoon faculty and students trickled in and out of the library during the hour between four to five o'clock, when tea was served. But today was different. The library was jam-packed by four-fifteen.

Alan Sidebottom, looking refreshed and cheerful, strode across the library to the tea table. Oblivious of the line of people waiting their turns, he approached the table directly and helped himself to a steaming cup of black tea with milk and two sugars. Mitchell Fender motioned for Alan to join Nedda Cake and himself. The three chatted amiably for a short while. There was a faint sheen of sweat on Mitchell's upper lip.

"I'm so sorry," Mitchell soon announced, leaping to his feet. "Must skedaddle—I have a tutorial in a few minutes. Alan, your cup is empty. I insist on getting you a refill before I scoot upstairs. Milk and sugar?"

"Thanks, old man," Alan said, holding out his cup and saucer.

Mitchell returned moments later with a fresh cup of steaming tea and gingerly handed it to Alan, careful not to spill any of the piping hot liquid.

"Righto then, see you both later!" Mitchell said, and hurried out of the library.

Nedda Cake turned to Alan Sidebottom.

"I must say, Alan, I'm impressed Mitchell has made such peace with you after that business about the plagiarism," she said. "Seems to be a habit with you."

Professor Sidebottom closed his eyes and took a long, slow sip of tea.

"Synchronous ideas happen all the time," he shrugged.

"But onto more important things, dear lady—how are *you*?" Professor Sidebottom said quickly. "How long has it been? You look marvelous, by the way. You've hardly changed at all. You must tell me all about your work!"

The two engaged in shoptalk, discussing various popular ideas of the day and carefully avoided any mention of their old days in Oxford. Neither mentioned Nedda's late husband, Frank Cake.

"May I?" Donald Gaylord interrupted, hovering next to a vacant chair with tea in hand.

"Sit down, dear boy," Professor Sidebottom said. "Do join us."

The three chatted together until five o'clock, joined at times by other faculty members, who would stay long enough for a bit of conversation and a cup of tea.

At the stroke of five o'clock, librarian Charlotte Cadell began packing up the tea table, and collected stranded cups and saucers from around the library. She glared sullenly at Alan Sidebottom at every chance, trying to attract his attention, but he appeared to take no notice of her.

Donald Gaylord stood to leave.

"Oh, Donald, before I forget," Alan Sidebottom said casually, "Tommy Walker said to say 'hello'. You remember Tommy."

Donald fumbled with his briefcase and accidentally dropped it. It hit the floor with a thud and opened, spilling the contents. Charlotte Cadell scurried over to help him gather up the scattered papers, shooting Professor Sidebottom an acid look.

"Oh, what a clumsy clod I can be!" Donald said, red-faced.

Across the library Edwina had been filling in her friends, Nate and Laura, on the events of Friday night when she escorted Alan Sidebottom back to the Carriage House after the party. Their curiosity piqued, and watching from a discreet distance, they had observed the professor throughout teatime. Although they witnessed what had just taken place with Donald Gaylord, they were too far away to hear what was said.

When Professor Sidebottom suddenly approached Edwina, Laura Brenner and Nate Harris, the three bumbled clumsily trying to appear nonchalant. Nate dropped a cookie on the floor, and he and Laura bumped heads leaning over to pick it up.

"Miss Goodman," Professor Sidebottom said to Edwina, "I wonder if you might be free for dinner this evening? I wanted to apologize for the other night."

Edwina's first thought was that dinner might be a repeat of the escapades of Friday night. She felt in an impossible situation. Nate and Laura, as if reading her mind, signaled their helplessness by smiling sheepishly.

"It's certainly not necessary, Professor," Edwina said, "but I would love to. How's six thirty? I'll meet you in town at The New World."

Donald Gaylord and Charlotte Cadell lingered unobtrusively, straightening out the papers from Donald's briefcase. They heard the exchange between Alan Sidebottom and Edwina, and were murmuring quietly between themselves.

After all overheard bits of other peoples' conversations really can't be helped in the graciously intimate surroundings of old Theodore Sanborn's cozy library. At least, that's what the collectors of gossip were telling themselves.

*

Edwina was one of the last people to leave Sanborn House as she headed out to meet Professor Sidebottom for dinner that night. She locked her office door and started down the hallway.

She was surprised to find Seth Dubin in the reception area, measuring out coffee for the coffee maker.

"You're working late, Seth," Edwina said.

"Oh, Edwina, hi—you surprised me," he said. "I thought everyone had pretty much left. Sheila's away for a couple of days. Figured I'd get in some extra work."

"I'm having dinner with Sidebottom. Why don't you join us?" Edwina said.

"Thanks for the offer. I've got a microwave dinner in the freezer waiting for me. Thanks, though. Have fun."

"See you tomorrow," Edwina replied.

*

The ambience in the New World Tavern was redolent of age and local history. Its low ceilings and creaking, uneven floorboards had stories to tell—stories of everyday, sometimes exciting, sometimes heroic, life in the colonies before America became the United States. Of course, the original meaning of the place was long gone. In the Darwinian way of survival, the tavern had evolved into something new—into a popular meeting place for lunch, dinner, and drinks, with students and swells alike. Its importance for once being a meeting place where crucial political discussions of the day took place had fallen by the wayside. That the old tavern was still thriving was remarkable.

The New World Tavern had been a fixture on the main thoroughfare in New Guilford since colonial times—part bar, part restaurant, part hotel, part stable— faithfully serving travelers and locals. The stable building out back was no longer there, but other original features remained, like the fireplace. Ten feet wide at its opening, the brick fireplace still had its small oven on the back wall, and a Dutch oven and toasting rack on the hearth floor. And the "cranes"—iron bars that held cooking pots from hooks and swung to and fro—were still in tact. The original taproom where cider and beer would have been served, as well as the small parlor where female travelers would have rested, had since been incorporated into the main dining room.

There had, of course, been other changes. In the 1940s a local artist and friend of the then proprietor painted murals on the inside walls. Toward the end of the artist's life his work started showing up in museums. Subsequently, the murals themselves had become a tourist destination and accordingly, were very well looked after. The insurance company had insisted on protective glass partitions in front of the murals. No longer an inn, the upstairs rooms were rented out as office space.

Edwina chose a booth with a good view of the murals. Her dinner companion instantly recognized the dab hand responsible for the bucolic scenes of farms and meadows.

"Do you know," he said, pointing toward an image in the foreground of a farmhouse and garden," when I was a boy I had a puss called 'Pudding'. She died from eating some of those purple flowers in the herbaceous border, there. They're deadly poisonous—the root, sap, stems, leaves, seeds—everything. We called them 'fairy fingers' when we were children."

Edwina studied the professor. His face reminded her of a Rembrandt self-portrait in a book—a beautiful and complicated map in light and shadow of the human spirit, showing all its strengths and vulnerabilities.

Alan Sidebottom looked at Edwina with a wry smile.

"Are you married, Edwina?" he asked.

"No. I don't think I've quite figured out how marriage and work fit together. "I did have a boyfriend for a while in grad school," she said.

"Serious?"

Edwina thought for a moment.

"Serious-ish," she answered. "He said I was 'prematurely absent-minded', because sometimes when he'd be talking, my mind would wander. I'd start turning over a mathematical problem in my head, and forget we were in the middle of a conversation. I'm sure it was incredibly annoying. He was actually a very nice guy. A geologist."

Professor Sidebottom chuckled.

"What about you? Are you married?" Edwina asked.

A deep chortle rumbled somewhere in his chest and came out as a sort of wheezy laugh.

"Well, let's see—I've been married for twenty-nine years, altogether. My first marriage lasted a year. She was a French girl I met on holiday—a lovely girl, named Marie-Laure. When I brought her back to England my brother seduced her. She fell in love with him, and they got married," Professor Sidebottom said.

"Did they stay together?" Edwina asked.

"Sickeningly, yes; they have four children and are madly devoted to each other," he said casually.

"A happy ending, then," Edwina said.

"Good lord, what do you people teach at Cushing? You must know by now that happy endings are a physical impossibility? There is simply no equation for it," the professor bantered.

"And after Marie-Laure?" Edwina said.

"Three more marriages. All failed."

"Why do you study physics?" he asked, starting on a second glass of scotch.

"Why not study physics?" she said. "It's the most interesting thing in the world. I often wonder why more people don't take it up, I really do. Once when I was a kid I visited an aquarium and spent the whole day staring at the air bubbles rising through a column of water. It was the liquid dynamics that interested me, not the fish. My parents had to drag me away."

Alan Sidebottom laughed.

"And another thing," Edwina continued. "Theoretical physicists make the best philosophers, don't you think so? I mean, who is better qualified to talk about the fundamental nature of reality than the people who know what the universe actually looks like?"

Professor Sidebottom beamed at her.

"Quite right!" he exclaimed, gulping down his third scotch.

After they ordered dinner the professor entreated Edwina to play a game of darts in the adjacent bar area. Edwina managed to persuade him that darts and drinking were a bad mix, and that someone could get hurt. He became immediately contrite, blushing deeply and begging her forgiveness for even suggesting it.   He burst into a heartfelt recitation of a love poem by Robert Burns, in perfect Scottish brogue.

"Ye flowery bands o' bonnie Doon,
How can ye blume sae fair!
How can ye chant, ye little birds,
And I sae fu' o' care!
Thou'll break my heart, thou bonnie bird,
That sings upon the bough;
Thou minds me o' the happy days
When my fause luve was true."

Professor Sidebottom had brought himself to tears with this recitation. He ordered a bottle of *prosecco* to quell his nerves.

"Do you know the stuff?" he said to Edwina. "No? We can't have that; you must try it! *Vino frizzante*— elixir to the gods, and all civilized people. You'll love it."

Anticipating another drunken scene Edwina wanted to go home, but she felt responsible for his safe return to campus. Forbearance and duty got the better of her until an hour later when Alan Sidebottom had finished the bottle *prosecco* by himself, and still hadn't touched his food. Edwina had had enough.

"I should probably get going," she said. "I have a pile of student papers to get through tonight."

Professor Sidebottom had recovered his high spirits. He paid the bill and left a large tip for their server, a college student who was clearly unnerved by Professor

Sidebottom's antics. Edwina guided her unsteady charge out of the restaurant, and they started back toward campus. She walked her bike with one hand and held onto Sidebottom's arm with the other.

He was grinning and muttering to himself. His dithering garble became intensified.

"Time I got the Barnet Fair hack toff!" he shouted.

Suddenly he broke away from Edwina and raced across the street, where he quickly disappeared down an alleyway.

Edwina grew instantly impatient and exasperated.

Fuck it, she thought. *"I'm not chasing after him."*

She stood on the spot and waited for him to return. Streetlights illuminated a pool of darkness around her, and reflected the marcasite chips in the pavement, making the sidewalk sparkle like glitter. The streets of New Guilford were mostly quiet.

Five minutes passed. Edwina got on her bicycle and headed home, feeling uneasy.

As she rode past the New Guilford Inn, a stylish country hotel and restaurant, the yellow incandescence from candlelit tables glowed invitingly and caught her eye. Glancing over, she peripherally glimpsed a woman who looked very much like Sheila Dubin, sitting at a corner table. The wide, canvas awning prevented a fuller view.

That's funny, she thought. *Seth said Sheila was out of town. Probably wasn't even her.*

Edwina considered circling back to see if it was Sheila or not, but she thought better of it and rode her bike toward home.

Enough drama for one night.

A few minutes later she changed her mind, curiosity getting the upper hand once again. With no cars in sight she made a U-turn in the quiet street, and pedaled back into town. Edwina stopped in the shadows, across the street from the New Guilford Inn, where she would not be visible. She stood straddling her bike, squinting to see the woman who resembled Sheila, but she could not find a good, clear angle. The corner table was obscured from her sight line.

The New Guilford Inn was situated in the middle of the block, sandwiched between buildings on either side. Edwina gingerly approached the Inn, walking her bike slowly alongside her through the shadows, trying to avoid stepping in the light from the streetlamp. She stopped at the end of the bank building, and peeked around the corner toward the Inn, which was set farther back from the sidewalk. Edwina rounded the corner of the bank and slowly inched along the sidewall of the bank, toward the Inn. Finally the corner table of the Inn's restaurant came into her field of vision. Edwina stood absolutely still in the shadows. She could now see the woman in question.

Sheila Dubin looked unusually glamorous. Shamelessly embracing the clichés of femininity she was dressed in a tight-fitting, red satin dress with a Mandarin collar and capped sleeves. The kind of tight-fitting that let people know she wasn't wearing undergarments. Her hair was fashioned into an up-do, and the candlelight glinted off her dangling earrings. The other side of the table was obscured from Edwina's view, and she dared not inch any closer, or she might be seen.

Edwina stood frozen, overcome by the naughty exhilaration of voyeurism. She noticed Sheila Dubin's lipstick matched the color of her dress, as did the polish on her fingernails. Sheila was glowing. After some minutes, her dinner companion reached across the table to refill her wine glass.

Donald Gaylord!

Edwina felt sick.

Poor Seth!

Edwina couldn't retreat quickly enough. She trotted her bike back up to the corner, where she crossed the street and sped off.

By the time she got home she was filled with feelings of doubt and anxiety.

.

Chapter 4

When Edwina arrived at Sanborn House the following day the whole place seemed to be at sixes and sevens. Staff and students were joined in hushed conversations on the stairway, in the library, in hallways. Librarian Charlotte Cadell was the first person Edwina saw.

"What's going on?" Edwina said with concern in her voice.

"Alan Sidebottom didn't show up for his seminar this morning!" Charlotte replied.

"Professor Mann called him but there was no answer, so she went over to the Carriage House. She could see him through the window, lying in bed, and she knocked on the door, thinking maybe he was sick or something, but Professor Sidebottom didn't respond. She called 9-1-1 and the paramedics came right away. Edwina, he was stone. Cold. Dead!" Charlotte pronounced dramatically.

Edwina struggled to take all of this in.

"But, I had dinner with him last night!" Edwina heard herself say. "What happened to him?"

"I don't know—I don't think they know, yet," Charlotte said, her eyes big with excitement. Fueled by adrenaline, her words tumbled out breathlessly, as if she felt titillated by the news.

Charlotte's demeanor struck Edwina as ghoulish.

Classes were cancelled for the day, but hardly anyone went home. Members of the teaching staff wandered aimlessly around the gloomy atmosphere of Sanborn House the rest of the day, drifting in and out of each other's offices, nosing around for more information. A bunch of whispering students spent the afternoon in the library, opting for gossip over study. There was a definite frisson in the air caused by the adventure of a death in their midst and the suspense of what might have caused it.

A text went around the Department after lunch inviting everyone to gather that evening at The New World. Surely the Department should band together in the wake of such tragedy.

*

At six o'clock students and staff from the Physics and Astronomy Department began trickling into The New World. The first few arrivals commandeered the only seating big enough to comfortably accommodate the group, a large, oval table in the front window bay.

In short order the entire department showed up. Drinks were ordered immediately. The mood was somber.

"I had dinner here with Professor Sidebottom *last night*," Edwina said incredulously. "It doesn't even seem real, now. How could he suddenly be gone? Doesn't make any sense. Especially somebody like that. So—I don't know—larger than life."

A waitress brought over a tray of drinks and handed them around.

"We all share those feelings," Seth Dubin offered quietly. "It's really difficult to take any of this in."

"I wonder if it could have been suicide?" graduate student Laura Brenner said.

"Yeah . . . I wonder if there was there a note?" chimed in fellow grad student Nate Harris.

This avenue of thought quieted the table momentarily as people considered the possibility of a suicide.

"Poor Alan was such an unhappy man, I think," Helen Mann said, draining a glass of red wine. "I believe there were a number of divorces—estrangements from children—the heavy drinking. Seems he made a mess of his personal life."

"Boy, what a waste," said first year instructor, Pete Talbot. "Such a brilliant mind."

"Not much point in our speculating about suicide or whatever else—we have so little information," said Nedda Cake. "The police will get to the bottom of it in due time."

"The police?" exclaimed Donald Gaylord, practically spitting out his malt whiskey.

"Of course, the police," Ravi Kapoor replied. "A man died. The circumstances must be looked into. Questions must be answered."

"But, I assumed it was natural causes. The man had a bad heart, and I mean, my God, all the drinking!" Donald said.

"You're probably right, Don. I imagine poor Alan had a heart attack in his sleep. It's probably just pro forma stuff as far as the police investigation goes," Seth Dubin said.

More drinks were ordered, and a few people ordered dinner. Mitchell Fender, never much of a drinker, was soon in his cups, and began to doze off.

"Here, Mitch," said Seth Dubin, gently rousing him. "Have half of my sandwich. It's huge. I can't possibly eat the whole thing."

Mitchell awoke with a start and ignored Seth's offer of half a sandwich. Instead, he raised his glass in a toast.

"The man was a drunk, a satyr, and a plagiarist," Mitchell said, tripping over his words. "But he didn't deserve to die. Rest in peace, you old horse thief!"

The table was quiet for a few moments. Professor Nedda Cake broke the uneasy silence.

"'Pride and grace ne'er dwelt in once place,'" Nedda said cryptically. "We live in a rather vast universe, and it's perhaps best to remember one's place in it. Alan was a very reckless man."

"That was beautiful, Nedda," Mitchell Fender said with tears in his eyes. "Pure poetry. You're an angel. You know? You really are. An angel."

A few sniggers were stifled around the table. Helen Mann discreetly asked the waitress to bring coffee for Mitchell. Seth Dubin patted Mitchell gently on the back and handed him a handkerchief.

"Do we know anything more about what happened?" asked Lois Lieberman.

There were murmurs around the table of general denial. No one had new information to offer.

Helen Mann spoke.

"The police said they would let me know when the cause of death is determined. It certainly seems like it will turn out to be a heart attack or maybe a stroke."

"It seems to me," Paolo Rossetti began, "that death, especially when it's so abrupt and unexpected has an abstract quality to it. It's as if our brains can't process the sudden end of existence. How could someone so alive suddenly be so absent? What has become of the essence of that individual? It's a frightening thing for us humans to contemplate, no?"

Charlotte Cadell spoke for the first time.

"But who's to say where the life force resides?" she said softly.

"Eh?" Mitchell Fender said.

"I was just wondering, Dr. Fender," Charlotte said graciously, "does the human spirit reside in the subatomic particles that make up our bodies and get recycled into the universe when we die? Or does it reside elsewhere? Does it even exist? Is Alan happier now, because his spirit can roam free, unencumbered by conscience or regret?"

Mitchell Fender blinked uncomprehendingly and reached for his bourbon.

For someone who barely knew Professor Sidebottom, Charlotte seems to have rare insight about him, Edwina thought, studying Charlotte's profile.

"My dear Charlotte!" said Donald Gaylord, "What a dark horse you are! I would never have dreamed such powers of reflection and perception lurked beneath that implacable lunar surface of yours!"

"Oh, shut it, Donald," Mitchell Fender snapped. "Do you always have to behave like such an effing singularity?"

"Charlotte is right!" Laura Brenner said. "What about all those people who report leaving their bodies in a near-death experience, and being able to observe themselves from outside their own bodies? How do we account for that?"

"Don't forget," Lois Lieberman interjected, "as Charlotte just pointed out, the very idea of physical reincarnation has some basis in physics."

"As physicists," said Paolo Rossetti, "we know there is more to the universe than meets the eye. We are dealing every day with forces we know exist, but that we cannot actually see or measure. Who are we to definitively rule out some of these possible scenarios?"

"Pish tosh!" Helen said dismissively, her lipstick slightly smeared. "There's no room for mysticism in science. Some of this palaver is alcohol talking!"

"I wonder if it's possible," said Charlotte Cadell, ignoring Helen, "that as astronomical observation becomes more powerful, and we are able to explore further into the universe—I wonder if scientists will bump into God one day and be able to prove his existence?"

"Or disprove it," said Paolo Rossetti.

Donald Gaylord rolled his eyes theatrically. Mitchell Fender looked as if he were about to implode.

Ravi Kapoor jumped in diplomatically.

"I'm sure we can all agree on one thing," Ravi said. "That is, that some things remain unknowable at the present time. There is room enough—and tolerance enough—for each to have his or her opinion, until such time as these questions are proven one way or the other."

"Well spoken, Ravi!" said Lois Lieberman.

Nearly everyone had ordered dinner by then, and the general conversation broke up into smaller groups around the table, when suddenly everyone's attention was directed toward Helen Mann.

Helen's eyes were no longer focusing sharply. Her usually impeccable appearance had started to fray. Her dark hair, which she wore in a short, smooth style resembling a helmet, had sprung a few loose strands, and her black eyeliner was traveling south. Slowly, Helen raised her fourth glass of red wine.

"'Man hath no better thing under the sun," she blurted out, "'than to eat, and to drink, and be merry'! And that's from the Bible, so drink up, god dammit! The Department is footing the tab for all this."

There were embarrassed murmurs of 'thank-you, Helen', and 'very generous of you, Helen' around the table. Only Nedda Cake ventured further.

"We're all very grateful for your generous gesture, Helen," Nedda said. "But this is perhaps not an occasion for merriment, seeing as there is one less among us today."

"So true, so true," Helen continued, speaking to her wine glass, "You know, I knew Alan Sidebottom thirty years ago. We met at a conference in Brussels. Alan seemed unhappy, even then, but he was so young, and so beautiful . . . I was young and beautiful, too." She glared around the table as if challenging anyone to disagree.

"We had a brief affair, couldn't keep our hands off each other, as a matter of fact."

The gathering sat silent. People looked down at their food. Laura Brenner nudged Edwina under the table. Helen Mann had always kept her personal life private, and the fact that she had divulged something so intimate while under the influence of alcohol was discomfiting to everyone. Except perhaps to Donald Gaylord, who relished Helen's confession with great satisfaction.

It was Seth Dubin who finally spoke, puncturing the moment.

"Tomorrow is another day, my friends. We all need to be fresh and rested in order to do our best work. What say we call it a night?"

Vastly relieved, most of the table got up to leave, mumbling 'good-night' or 'see you tomorrow'. A few straggled behind. Edwina couldn't get out of the restaurant fast enough, unsettled as she felt by practically everything that had happened since she arrived at Sanborn House that morning.

She jumped on her bike and started home, happy for the fresh air to clear her head. When she got to her little house on Canaan Farm Road she washed up and went to bed, and quickly fell into a deep sleep, laden with dreams she could not, would not, remember the next day.

*

Edwina woke up the next morning with a heavy feeling of guilt over Alan Sidebottom's death. She could not shake off the notion that she had been somehow delinquent. That it was somehow her fault Sidebottom had met with an untimely ending. After all, she had been with him earlier on the very night he died.

She hardly knew what to do with these feelings, so she busied herself in the kitchen making breakfast, fed logs into the wood stove and stoked the fire. She filled the kettle with water, set it on top of the wood stove, and sat down at the kitchen table in her nightgown. Outside the window a group of chickadees perched patiently on the branches of an apple tree, while a spirited gang of blue jays monopolized the bird feeder, squawking and carrying on like drunken frat boys.

 Edwina picked at a breakfast of oatmeal, toast with orange marmalade, and tea, while she watched the birds outside the window, all the while thinking about Alan Sidebottom. Finches, juncos and sparrows joined the chickadees, waiting for their turns at the feeder. When six crows suddenly swooped onto the scene, the blue jays screamed bloody murder, flapping their wings wildly.

Wasn't that typical of bullies, to raise the alarm when they become the bullied, Edwina thought.

With no classes to teach until the following morning, Edwina felt like taking the day off. Maybe pack a lunch and go kayaking. Maybe just sit in the rocker of her cozy kitchen, feeding sweet-smelling wood into the wood-stove and watching the birds. She gazed across the room at the stack of student papers piled high on the kitchen table. She leaned her head back in the rocking chair and closed her eyes, certain in the knowledge that she would spend the entire day carefully reading through every one of them, and giving considered thought to the comments she would write in the margins. Emitting a sighing little moan, she rearranged herself in the wicker rocking chair by the window, and concentrated on the ongoing drama at the birdfeeder for ten more minutes.

Chapter 5

Chief of Police Valerie Burnstein was nursing a headache.

The New Guilford Police Department had not had a suspicious death on its hands in years, and Chief Val, a pleasant-looking, middle-aged woman who had pictures of her grandchildren on her desk, was feeling put out. She was looking forward to retirement in two years, and in recent times had gotten lulled into the quiet routine of nothing more serious than shoplifters or people writing bad checks.

Detective William Tenney handed her his report, and sat down across the desk.

"What the hell kind of retirement joke is this, Will?" she muttered, reading through the report and sipping coffee from an 'I Heart Grandma' mug.

"No blood at the scene," she read, "no sign of a struggle, no injuries. No forced entry. Nothing missing, that we know of. Who is he?"

"Alan Anthony Sidebottom. A physics professor from Cambridge, England, teaching at Cushing this semester," Will said.

"Jesus, poor guy," Chief Val said. "Looks like he'd only been here a few days. Some welcome. Have you contacted the family?"

"I reached a sister late last night. She's flying over tomorrow. And I spoke with the head of the department here at Cushing, a Dr. Helen Mann. She was plenty shook up."

"There was digoxin at the scene," Chief Val read, "with his name on the prescription, so he had a heart condition. He could have died of a heart attack in his sleep."

"Possible," said Will. "We'll know a whole lot more when we get the coroner's report."

"Find me some Advil, would you, Will?" the Chief said, rubbing her forehead.

*

Detective William Tenney, aged thirty-two, was a hard-working, solitude-loving New England Yankee, like his father, a country doctor. Will's mother, Cecile, was a classical musician, and had grown up in Paris. She and Will's father met in New York when Cecile was studying at Julliard and Will's father was interning at Mt. Sinai Hospital.

Cecile's parents—Will's grandparents—had fled to England in 1939, before finally being able to move back to their native France at the end of the war. The stories his grandparents told him had impressed Will deeply as a boy, and instilled in him a desire to become a protector of those in need of protecting.

Will's parents had offered him in a simple formula for happiness. Find out what you love to do, they instructed him, carve out a niche where you can do it, and then try to improve your little corner of the world. *Imagine if everyone did that,* his mother used to say.

Will was engaged in the pleasurable activity of building a house for himself on a secluded piece of land twelve miles outside New Guilford. The majority of his spare time went into this project. He enlisted the help of friends only when he needed to—for the laying of the foundation, for instance—but much of the work he could manage alone, and he preferred it that way. Like

Edwina, Will was an only child. Self-reliance was something of a religion with him.

The two-story clapboard house would have an open interior—one big living space—with stairs leading to a sleeping loft area. He had recently completed construction on the stone chimney and fireplace that would eventually heat the whole house. He hoped to have the roof completed before the first heavy snowfall, and it looked like he would be on schedule.

For the time being, Will had erected a tipi on the property, twenty-four feet in diameter, where he lived during construction on the house. He bathed in a spring-fed pond on the property. Reactions of his family and friends to this arrangement ranged from worried concern to stark envy. Will paid little attention to any of it.

*

Will was doing paper work when Chief Val called him into her office.

"Got the coroner's report back," she said. "Alan Sidebottom died from a heart attack caused by digitalis poisoning," she read.

"We know he was taking digoxin for a heart condition," she continued, "but now we know his blood alcohol was point-one-four. I'm thinking that maybe he took too many of his pills by mistake—when he was drunk—and passed away in his sleep."

Will nodded thoughtfully.

"What about suicide?" he asked.

"Possible," Chief Val replied. "I want you to canvas the folks at the college. Ask around the department," she paused to glance at the report, "Physics and Astronomy. See if you can get anything on whether he was depressed or upset about something, or recently divorced or in financial trouble—"

"Got it," said Will.

*

Detective Will Tenney drove through downtown New Guilford—described in guidebooks as 'picturesque' and 'quaint'—past white-trimmed, brick buildings with green awnings, shop windows with tidy flowerboxes and clean sidewalks, and an abundance of bicycle racks. Main Street appeared dozy at the moment but it would be bustling by lunchtime.

Will parked his official police vehicle in a visitor's area of the parking lot behind the Cushing College administration building. He set out for Sanborn House along the pedestrian path that wound for miles through the bucolic college grounds. As Will passed by a low, glass and concrete classroom building nestled alongside a row of ivy-covered, Georgian brick buildings, he noted appreciatively how harmoniously the old architecture mixed in with the new.

Will ascended the steps of Sanborn House, home to the Physics and Astronomy Department, and was greeted at the top by a pair of lions carved in stone, flanking the main entrance. He pulled open a heavy wooden door, and entered the main vestibule, which was dominated by a massive marble staircase. The directory told him reception and staff offices were on the second floor.

There was no one sitting at the desk in the spacious reception area at the top of the stairs. Hallways at the north and south end of this area led to offices. Will started down one hallway in search of Alan Sidebottom's office.

A plaque reading, 'Prof. A. Sidebottom' appeared on a door halfway down the long hallway. It was unlocked. Will let himself inside, closing the door behind him. Bare bookshelves and an empty desktop awaited the new tenant. The only sign of occupancy was a half-filled wire mesh wastebasket.

Will sat down at the desk and pulled the wastebasket toward him. The contents included a packet of coupons from local shops; a notification from the public library of upcoming events; an invitation from a classical music society; and an advertisement for a month's free membership at a gym. Will opened the desk drawers and found nothing other than a few stray paper clips.

Will stood by the window and surveyed the scene, his view partially obscured by a mature maple tree. The pedestrian path was intermittently visible through its branches. He watched the students hurrying along the path, cheerful, buoyed by the certainty of happy lives ahead. The thought popped into his head that Alan Sidebottom was once just like them.

*

Will closed the door to Professor Sidebottom's office and continued along the hallway. The name on the next door was that of Donald Gaylord. He knocked.

"Come in," Donald called.

Will entered the neat and well-appointed office to find Donald Gaylord working at his desk. He looked up, and seeing Will, closed the computer.

"Yes?" Donald said.

"Donald Gaylord? I'm Detective William Tenney from the New Guilford Police Department. May I ask you a few questions about Alan Sidebottom?" he said, showing identification.

"What?" Professor Gaylord said, startled. "Oh, of course, the Sidebottom business. Please, sit down."

Framed photographs of Donald Gaylord playing college football were hung artfully along one wall. Books took up the rest of the wall space. The orderly desk displayed a single photograph in a silver frame of a handsome young woman, alongside a Victorian inkwell set with two glass inkwells in an ebonized wood tray.

"Your wife, sir?" the detective asked, regarding the photo.

"Yes, my wife," Donald Gaylord said. "What can I do for you, detective?"

"We're making enquiries about Alan Sidebottom. I'll be speaking with everyone in the department. I wonder if you can tell me anything about his short stay here at Cushing?"

"How do you mean?" Professor Gaylord replied.

"For instance, were you acquainted with him before he came to Cushing? Do you know anything about his personal life? Can you shed any kind of light on his untimely death?"

"No, not really," Professor Gaylord said, folding his hands in his lap. "I'm sorry, but I don't think I have anything to offer the investigation. I mean, I can tell you that his reputation preceded him. And, of course, I have read all of his books. I think most of us around here have."

Will gazed coolly at Professor Gaylord, his curiosity provoked by Gaylord's fidgety evasiveness.

"Had you met him before he arrived at Cushing?" Will repeated.

"Well, yes, as a matter of fact. I did meet Alan about eighteen years ago, when I was doing undergraduate work at Cambridge for a time. I took one of Alan's seminars."

Christ, I'd call that being acquainted! Will thought.

"Were you in touch with him during the years in between?"

"No. I kept up with Dr. Sidebottom's work over the years, but we had no personal contact."

"We think Professor Sidebottom died in his sleep from a heart attack. We're looking into what might have caused it. Do you know of any reason he might have been unusually stressed or depressed? Had he had a shock of any kind?"

Professor Donald Gaylord fiddled with a silver letter opener fashioned to look like an arrow.

"N—no—not really. I mean, anyone will tell you that Alan, although brilliant and highly respected in our field, was probably not universally well-liked . . ."

"Meaning?"

"I don't wish to speak ill of the dead, detective. I really don't. It's just that he had a bit of a reputation— for philandering and plagiarism, among other things. As such, he alienated any number of people. Maybe someone confronted him? I expect something like that could bring on a heart attack. And, of course, lots of people in the field had reason to be jealous of Alan. Of his fame and success, and so on. That may have been upsetting for him as well."

"Care to be more specific, sir?"

Professor Gaylord cleared his throat.

"One doesn't wish to tell tales. But there was quite a commotion last year when Professor Sidebottom published a book that some of us felt borrowed heavily from Mitchell Fender's work on black holes. Perhaps meeting Mitchell face to face activated Alan's conscience. I would certainly want to speak to Mitchell Fender if I were you."

Will made notes but said nothing. He knew Donald Gaylord was not done spilling. The guy was on a roll.

"Nedda Cake had reason to be angry with Alan, as well, come to think of it. Nedda is the senior member of our department; she's almost ninety. Alan was a student of Dr. Cake's late husband many years ago in England. The story goes that Alan drove Old Professor

Cake to an early grave when he plagiarized some of his work. Perhaps Alan had an attack of conscience about that, seeing Nedda again."

Will sat back in his chair and nodded encouragement, hoping for more.

"There's Seth Dubin, of course. He's a gifted young physicist, certain to get tenure here at Cushing—mild-mannered, a nice man. The night of the cocktail party to welcome Alan into our merry cadre, Alan behaved horribly toward Seth. Actually made fun of his stammer, mocked the poor man. I don't know how Professor Sidebottom felt about the encounter, but Seth Dubin certainly had cause for being greatly upset. Not to mention Seth's wife, whom I'm told felt deeply humiliated by the whole incident."

"Told by whom, sir?"

"I beg your pardon?"

"You were told that Mrs. Dubin was upset and humiliated by Professor Sidebottom's mocking behavior toward her husband. Who happened to tell you that?"

Donald straightened his tie.

"You know, I believe it was Mrs. Dubin, herself, who told me," Donald said.

"Anything else come to mind, sir?"

"Not at the moment, no," Professor Gaylord said. "But if I think of anything . . . oh, and I'd appreciate being kept apprised, as the investigation goes along."

"In due course, sir. Thank you for your time. And please do get in touch if you think of anything else," Will said, placing his card on Donald Gaylord's uncluttered desk.

*

Edwina, dressed in jeans and a flowery, button-down shirt, could almost see over the top of the armload of books she was carrying. But not quite. As Will exited Donald Gaylord's office, she collided with him.

"Sorry!" Will exclaimed, squatting down to pick up the books. "I didn't see you coming,"

"That's okay," Edwina replied. "It was my fault; I couldn't see where I was going."

Will stacked the books neatly and gathered them in his arms.

"Where to?" he asked.

"Oh, thanks. End of the hall, on the left," she replied.

Edwina unlocked the door to her small office, and Will followed her inside.

"Thanks again—would you put them right here?" she said, clearing a space on her desk.

Will set the books down carefully, and the two stood looking at each other for an awkward moment.

A constellation of pale freckles across Edwina's nose and cheeks held Will's attention, as did her faint smell of wood smoke. He wondered why this student had her own office. After some moments Will realized he was staring at her.

"William Tenney," he said proffering a hand. "I'm a detective with the New Guilford Police. We're looking into the death of Alan Sidebottom."

"Edwina Goodman," she replied, motioning for Will to sit down.

"Are you—do you teach here?"

"I look too young, you mean," Edwina laughed. "I get that all the time. I do teach, yeah. I finished my doctorate last year, and now I teach beginning level courses in physics, along with doing research."

 Will nodded.

"How did Professor Sidebottom die?" she asked.

"Heart attack."

"It's so terrible. I feel awful about it, especially since I was with Professor Sidebottom the night he died," she said.

"Oh?"

"Yes, I was having dinner with him at the New World Tavern on Monday night, the night before Professor Mann found him at the cottage."

"Was it, like, a date?"

"No, not exactly," Edwina said. "Donald Gaylord asked me to escort Professor Sidebottom home after the party we had Friday night at the library. That was the day he arrived at Cushing. As a matter of fact, Professor Gaylord picked him up at the airport, and brought him straight to the party. Well, no, that's not quite true. Professor Gaylord told me that Professor Sidebottom insisted on stopping somewhere for a drink on the way from the airport. He was pretty drunk by the time they got to Sanborn House, and Professor Gaylord seemed incredibly annoyed about it."

"Anyway, I was telling you that Professor Sidebottom was going to be staying at the Carriage House, which is a little guest cottage on campus where the college puts up visiting scholars and people like that. VIPs and stuff. It's just a few minutes walk from Sanborn House, but Professor Sidebottom had even more to drink at the party. As I was walking with him to the cottage, he passed out drunk," Edwina explained.

"He fainted during the course of a few minutes walk from Sanborn House to the Carriage House?" Will repeated, making notes.

"Yes. As I say, he really had a lot to drink. He sort of tripped and fell into the hedge, threw up, and passed out."

"Good Lord."

"I checked his pulse to make sure he wasn't dead. Then, luckily, a couple of students came along, and they helped me carry him to the cottage. We got him onto the bed and covered him up."

"And then?"

"Then I locked up and left."

"Right," said Will, taking more notes. "Tell me about this dinner the two of you had."

"Let's see. Monday afternoon at tea Professor Sidebottom invited me to dinner, as a way of apologizing for what happened Friday night. I didn't really want to go, for the very good reason that it could happen all over again, which it did," she said.

"After dinner—which he didn't eat a single bite of— I figured I had better walk him back to campus, because he was drunk again, and I felt responsible for getting him back safely," she continued. "All of a sudden as we were walking up Main Street, he just bolted. Took off running before I knew what was happening. I was amazed he could move that fast, with all that alcohol in him."

"Did he say anything?"

"You mean, to me?"

"Well, to you, or to anybody. Did he say anything in particular you can remember, before he ran off?"

"As we were walking up Main Street, he was sort of mumbling to himself. I remember feeling a little self-conscious because he looked like some homeless guy, with his wild hair and eccentric way of dressing— stumbling along—you know, muttering to himself and everything."

"Eccentric way of dressing?" Will interrupted.

"Well, country squire sort of stuff, but with a twist. Like, tweeds and sweater vests and long neck scarves, with sandals and socks."

Will smiled. Edwina looked out the window.

"I feel guilty about what happened," she said. "I keep thinking that if I had been at the cottage—if I had chased him down and taken him home—this might not have happened."

"What happened when Professor Sidebottom ran off? Did you call out to him, or try to run after him?" Will said.

"That's just it," Edwina sighed. "I feel terrible saying this, but the truth is that I was fed up with him. With the drinking and falling down and throwing up. I assumed it was more or less a way of life for him, and I figured he would be able to get back to campus on his own, so I waited for about five minutes, and then I left and went home."

"Do you live on campus?" asked Will.

" I live on Canaan Farm Road."

"How did you get home that night?"

"On my bike. That's how I get everywhere."

Will made more notes.

Edwina reached into a desk drawer and removed a rectangular tin box. She pried off the lid and held the box out to Will.

"Have one. Professor Cake baked them, homemade shortbread cookies."

"Thank-you," said Will.

The two sat in silence, watching each other chewing, waiting for the other to speak.

"Did Professor Sidebottom seem preoccupied or worried about anything in particular during dinner?" Will asked.

Edwina thought for a moment.

"I wish I could be more helpful, but no—nothing very serious came up in our conversation. I think he had a pretty complicated life . . . who knows how much of the gossip is true, but there were a lot of stories flying around about him."

"Such as?"

"Well, as I say, this is gossip and rumor, now. Not fact. I can tell you what I've heard on the grapevine, but I don't know what's true and what isn't," Edwina replied.

"Stuff like plagiarism, affairs with married women, smashing up a bookstore window, estrangements from his children, flings with students—things like that. Enough to put a strain on your heart, I would imagine, especially on top of all that drinking."

"We haven't ruled out suicide."

"Suicide?" Edwina frowned. "Oh, no, I don't see that at all. Professor Sidebottom was full of life. He was a very vital person. In his own pickled way."

She took another bite of cookie.

"If anything," she continued, crumbs falling onto her shirt, "I would guess he'd been murdered. According to some of the stories, he had a knack for making enemies, and—oh! I've just remembered something! Something very weird just popped into my head—it's what Professor Sidebottom said before he ran away that night!"

Edwina closed her eyes and pushed her bangs to one side, trying to recall the arcane utterance.

"Time for the Barnet Fair hat-toss," she said slowly. "It was something like that, anyway. Sorry, I'm not positive."

Will wrote it down in his notebook.

There was a knock at the door.

"Come in," Edwina called.

Bishop Larkin walked into the small office. He looked at Edwina and then at Will, and back at Edwina.

"Come on in, Bish," Edwina said.

"I'll just be going," Will said.

"Thank you for your help. And for the cookie. If you think of anything else, would you call me?" Will said handing her his card.

Chapter 6

Edwina was too worked up thinking about the case to get any work done.

If only I could figure out what Professor Sidebottom meant before he ran off, she thought. *On the other hand, what if it was just drunken gibberish that didn't mean anything at all?*

Edwina flipped open her laptop and made a few idle searches, looking for information about Alan Sidebottom that might shed more light on the investigation. Nothing new jumped out at her.

She turned her attention to the window. She gazed outside and let her thoughts run wild, without censoring or redirecting any snippet of thought that came to mind, just free-associating.

She turned her focus back to the Internet, and typed in a new search. Staring at the screen intently, she began to grow excited. After a few minutes she snapped the computer shut, flew out of the office and raced downstairs.

Sanborn House was connected to the main library in Hinley Hall by way of an underground passageway. Another of Theodore Sanborn's innovations, the subterranean passageway provided an indoor short cut during the harsh New England winter months when the landscape was covered in snow and ice.

Edwina walked quickly through the passageway and came out in the lower level of Hinley Hall, where a catacomb of cavernous rooms housed the library's closed 'stacks'. These books were available to librarians, only. Library patrons put in requests for books at the front desk on the main floor, and librarians retrieved the titles from the tens of thousands of volumes arranged in bookshelves in the closed stacks.

Edwina bounded up the staircase to the main floor, taking two steps at a time. After consulting the computerized card catalogue, she put in her book requests at the front desk, and waited. Within ten minutes the books were in her hands.

Edwina checked out two books on British rhyming slang and returned with them via the passageway to Sanborn House, reading along the way. Her suspicion regarding the meaning of Alan Sidebottom's strange utterance was growing stronger, but she would have to wait until later to study the books more thoroughly. Edwina had a class to teach, and her students came first. Her private search into Alan Sidebottom's death would have to be put on hold for the moment.

Edwina had late night duty in the lab at Sanborn House that evening, doing research. She let herself into the darkened building with a key, and flipped on the light switch near the staircase. Edwina was responsible for collecting data in a research project, and she had fallen behind because of the Sidebottom inquiry. She was intent on getting caught up, however long it might take, as it would have been unforgivable to jeopardize the outcome of the project out of simple neglect.

She had forgotten to eat dinner before arriving at the lab, and, inevitably, she was eventually interrupted by the noise of her grumbling stomach and accompanying light-headedness. She looked at her watch.

"What? It can't be ten o'clock already!" she exclaimed.

She scrabbled around in her backpack and found a granola bar, which she gratefully devoured. Still hungry, she ventured downstairs from the third floor to the reception area on the second floor, which functioned as a sort of common room. Hoping to find something that could pass for dinner, Edwina rifled through the bottles of juice and iced tea in the mini-refrigerator under the coffee maker and discovered two containers of strawberry yogurt. She guzzled the sweet, creamy yogurt, and made a mental note of the brand and flavor, which she would replace the following day.

Edwina started back up the stairs to the lab on the third floor, and settled back in at the computer. When she next looked at her watch it was one thirty in the morning.

Might as well sleep over, she thought. *I'm too tired to ride home, and anyway, it won't be the first time!*

She removed a toothbrush and toothpaste from her backpack and walked down the corridor to the Ladies' Room. Washed and brushed for the night, she turned off the lights in the lab, and went back downstairs to the second floor. She kicked off her shoes and flopped down on a comfortable sofa in the reception area, covering herself with her fleece jacket. Lulled by the soft ticking of a grandfather clock, she quickly fell to sleep.

A few hours later Edwina was awakened by the sound of voices. Startled and momentarily confused by her surroundings, she sat up and stayed very still. What sounded like two voices, a man's and a woman's, drifted faintly from one of the offices.

Edwina tiptoed toward the direction of the voices. The whole place was in pitch dark, and she had to creep along slowly through the reception area, to avoid bumping into anything or tripping. When she got to the hallway it was too dark to make out the names on the doors. The darkness was disorienting and it was difficult to gauge where she was.

Edwina hovered in the hallway, breathless, heady with curiosity. With no escape plan in mind, and no adequate explanation for spying if she got caught, she simply hoped the office door would not suddenly open. She was determined to know whose voices she was hearing.

Edwina could not make out the hushed words being exchanged, but she gleaned intonations of anger and recrimination. She thought the male voice might be Donald Gaylord. The female voice sounded familiar, too, but she could not quite place it. She had definitely heard it before.

Starting to feel nervous about getting caught, Edwina reached down into the pockets of her jeans trying not to make a sound. She felt around for a scrap of paper or a rubber band or paper clip. Gingerly, she extracted a lone toothpick. Silently, she bent down to feel for the baseboard along the wall, and carefully laid the toothpick on its narrow ledge. She backtracked to her own office as hastily as she could, and slept fitfully for the rest of the night on two chairs pulled together.

She awoke the next morning at seven o'clock with a stiff neck. It was too early for the department secretary, Ruth Benjamin, to be at her desk in Reception, so Edwina ducked into the Ladies' Room. She washed her face, combed her hair, and brushed her teeth, hoping no one would suspect she had slept over. Remembering the toothpick, she walked quickly down the hallway to retrieve it.

Sure enough, there it was, sitting atop the baseboard trim right outside Donald Gaylord's office.

*

Will Tenney felt somewhat intimidated by Professor Helen Mann. Her height of six feet did nothing to discourage the Head of the Physics and Astronomy Department from wearing preposterously high heels, and the result was that she towered over most people— even Will, who was also six feet tall. Helen's helmet-hairstyle, sharp nose, and prominent incisor teeth conjured an almost predatory appearance.

Helen welcomed the detective into her office, and gave him a firm handshake. She sat down in a Queen Anne wingback chair behind her massive desk.

"How can I help you, detective?"

"Thank-you for meeting with me," he said. "The New Guilford Police Department is looking into the death of Alan Sidebottom. I'd like to ask you a few questions, if you don't mind."

"Not at all," Helen replied.

"How long have you been Head of the department?"

"Ten years," she said. "I was appointed when Professor Jacobson retired.

"Did you know Alan Sidebottom well?"

"Not well, no. We hadn't spoken in decades. I won't mince words with you, detective; I knew Alan in the Biblical sense. But that was some thirty years ago, and we did not maintain any kind of relationship afterward. It was a brief affair, one of those things one does when one is young and foolish."

Will kept quiet, taking notes and waiting for more information. Helen merely returned his gaze. This standoff lasted for almost a minute, each trying to take the measure of the other.

"Is there anything you can tell me that might help with the investigation? Anything that might shed light on Professor Sidebottom's untimely death?" Will prodded. "Problems he might have been having with a student, or a fellow teacher? Any problems in his personal relationships?"

Helen shifted uncomfortably in her chair, and accidentally knocked some papers off the desk. Will picked them up off the floor and handed them to her. On top was a pink flyer advertising a discount for a haircut.

"I could do with a haircut, myself," he said genially. "Is this place any good?"

"I wouldn't know. I go to Boston to get my hair done. Makes a nice change from small town life," Helen explained imperiously.

"Can you tell me whose decision it was to invite Alan Sidebottom to Cushing?" Will asked.

"It was mine, as a matter of fact. I felt it would be very good for the department's standing to have someone as prominent as Alan Sidebottom teaching here for the semester. Alumni love that sort of thing. Famous names associated with the college seem to encourage them to contribute more money to the old alma mater. And we always need more money. Simple fact of life. Running a financially successful department is what I get paid for, detective."

"Had you been in touch with Professor Sidebottom at all over the years? Had you seen him in the past thirty years?" Will asked.

"No. We fell completely out of touch," Helen replied.

"Did you harbor ill will toward him because of your earlier relationship?"

"Not at all," Helen said. "I chalked it up to youthful folly. Nothing more, nothing less."

Will made notes. He felt sure Helen Mann was being less than completely honest. Her presumptive royalty act was getting on his nerves. But more than that, he knew she acted that way as a defense. She was hiding something about herself or about Alan Sidebottom's death. Or both.

"It seems that Professor Sidebottom led a very colorful life," Will said. "From what I understand he had any number of enemies."

"If you're talking about the situation with Mitchell Fender, it's old news. I had a talk with Mitch about it before Alan Sidebottom arrived. The whole incident was put to rest. Mitchell gave me his word that he would not stir up any old business that might create divisiveness in the department," Helen said. "And Mitch knows I mean business."

"Uh-huh. Well, thank you for your time, Dr. Mann. If you do think of anything else, please give me a call," Will said, leaving his card.

Chapter 7

Ravi Kapoor was the first one to arrive at the Observatory that evening. He parked his car in the deserted parking area, and crunched his way across the gravel courtyard, looking upwards at the moonless, black sky, stuffed full of gleaming constellations. The sound of his footsteps was amplified in the surrounding silence.

The shadowy, cavernous spaces inside the Observatory aroused in Ravi a sense of awe and wonder from his childhood, just as if it were his very first visit to the planetarium. Never had a place moved him so deeply. Never had architecture registered on him as something sacred, the way the building soared upwards toward the heavens and seemed to touch the sky. Here was Ravi's cathedral.

He passed through the darkened, domed room where the telescope was housed, into the computer control room. Ravi took off his coat, flipped on the lights, and settled in at the computer console. He soon heard someone enter the building.

"Lois not here, yet?" Paolo Rossetti said, appearing in the doorway.

"No," Ravi said, looking up. "That's kind of weird. She's usually the first one here," he said, checking his watch.

Their brief preliminaries over, the conversation turned to the subject at hand of theoretical cosmology and to the data they were analyzing.

A text rang on Ravi's phone.

"Lois says she can't make it," Ravi said. "She's not feeling well."

"Anything serious?" Paolo said.

"Tummy bug," replied Ravi.

*

Lois Lieberman did feel a bit sick to her stomach, but it was because she had lied to Ravi and Paolo, something she had never done before, and something so out of character she vowed never to do it again.

But desperate times called for desperate measures, and Lois was desperately in love with a married man who had called in the late afternoon to say he could see her that evening if she could get free.

Lois disliked the subterfuge and the questionable morality of her situation intensely. But when human wiring goes right, the impulse to endure outweighs all else, and Lois rationalized her affair with the belief that her paramour could only be happy with her, and she with him, and that without one another each would suffer. In the urge to thrive, all bets were off.

The man parked his car two blocks away from Lois's house. He walked the rest of the way under cover of darkness, through the unlit, sleepy streets. Lois let him in the kitchen door at the back of the house where they would not be observed.

"It's getting late," Paolo said, looking at his watch. "I think I'll call it a night. How about you?"

"I think I'll stay a bit longer," Ravi said, staring at the computer screen. "I am very encouraged by this data—I just want to look at a bit more. See you tomorrow."

"Ciao, Ravi. See you in the morning."

Paolo zipped his coat against the cold night air, and on the way to his car had a sudden thought.

Poor Lois and her stomach bug! I'll pick up some ginger ale and plain crackers and chamomile tea on the way home, and leave a care package at her door, Paolo thought, filled with the satisfaction of having thought up a good deed for a friend.

*

Paolo parked his car on the quiet street in front of Lois's house, since he did not wish to wake her with the sound of his car pulling into the driveway. He scribbled a note and stuck it inside the bag of grocery items. Carefully setting the bag on the wrought iron bench next to the front door Paolo began a silent retreat back to his car.

Just as he turned away from the house he caught a brief movement out of the corner of his eye. He focused on the upstairs window where he thought the movement came from, and stood still, waiting to see if anything else would happen. No light came on. All was quiet.

Perhaps it was nothing, Paolo thought.

Anyway, I'd better get home before Francesca starts to worry about me.

*

Will stopped by Sanborn House, hoping to interview the librarian. A dozen students sat scattered at long, library tables, reading and studying, working at laptops, even napping. Others had settled into comfy reading chairs in recessed alcoves that overlooked the college Green. The atmosphere in the library was tranquil and quiet.

Will found Charlotte Cadell hovering over the tea table, arranging rows of sliced cake, scones and cookies on a Calyx ware platter.

At some point during her seventeen years at Cushing College, Charlotte Cadell had managed to carve out the Physics and Astronomy library at Sanborn House as her undisputed territory. This meant that no one – not even Heads of Department – quibbled with her about anything to do with how the library was run. Over the course of her stewardship the library evolved into something of Charlotte's personal principality – rules governing the library were proposed and enacted by her, alone.

Although no one could remember quite how this de facto arrangement came to be, it was widely respected. Occasionally misled by Charlotte's demure demeanor, and by the idea that they outranked her, a few department members along the way had made the mistake of being high-handed with her, or of questioning her authority. Charlotte knew when and how to be quietly ferocious, and these missteps were rarely repeated.

Having finished arranging the tea table Charlotte sat down at her desk and tucked her skirt tautly under her thighs. In her forties, she displayed the dull remnants of what was once natural beauty. She was one of those attractive women who made little or no effort toward her appearance. On occasion she wore a bit of lipstick, but no more than that. Her butterscotch-color hair was graying, and her once lovely figure had thickened at the waistline. Charlotte Cadell's delicate features and fine bone structure told the story of classic, faded beauty, like the portrait of a beautiful woman, slightly blurred and discolored by sunlight.

Will observed her for some moments before approaching.

"Miss Cadell? May I have a word?" Will showed her his identification.

"How can I help?" she said.

"Is there somewhere more private we can sit and talk?"

"Of course; let's go up top," Charlotte smiled graciously.

Will followed her up a spiral staircase at the far end of the library. They emerged onto a balcony rimmed with floor-to-ceiling, glass-fronted bookcases and a smattering of reading chairs. Sunlight streamed onto the patterned carpet through a large arched window.

"We are investigating the death of Alan Sidebottom. Since you are in charge of the library, I thought you might be in a unique position to observe departmental goings-on," Will said. "Any information at all would be helpful."

"You mean, gossip I might have overheard?" she smiled coyly, raising her eyebrows at Will.

Will returned her cool gaze and did not answer.

"I can tell you that Dr. Fender disliked Alan Sidebottom intensely, for plagiarizing his work," Charlotte said. "It's common knowledge. But Mitchell Fender is a good and decent man, and would never hurt anyone. So I think that's probably a non-lead."

Will nodded encouragement and took notes.

"A bunch of us got together the evening after Professor Sidebottom died. Everyone was so upset. Dr. Dubin was his usual, kind self, making sure everybody else was doing okay, you know? I thought Dr. Cake was kind of quiet. It was amazing, the things people said—*in vino veritas,* you know. I was awfully interested—along with everybody else—to find out that Dr. Mann knew Alan a long time ago, and had an affair with him. I don't think she meant to blurt that out. I think she had had too much to drink, and it just slipped out. And I remember that Dr. Gaylord seemed on edge that night. I can't think why that would be. Poor Dr.

Fender had too much to drink, too, and behaved rather foolishly . . . I don't know what more I can tell you."

Will finished writing and set his notepad and pen on his lap.

"That's a very pretty ring, Miss Cadell," he said. "My mother had one very much like it. If I remember right, the stones spell out a message from the giver to the receiver—Victorian, isn't it?"

"Y-yes. Yes, it is."

"Let me see if I can work yours out—that's a fire opal, isn't it?—onyx—rose quartz—garnet—don't know that stone—don't know this one, either—and last but not least, an emerald. F-O-R-G-something—something—E. Would it be, 'forgive'?"

Miss Cadell was silent. She stared down at the ring she had not taken off her finger for eighteen years.

"This stone is iolite, and this one is vendite, so yes; you're right," she said in a soft voice. "I was engaged a long time ago. He gave me this ring as an apology, when things didn't work out."

"I'm sorry to hear it," Will said. "Where is he now?"

"He died in a climbing accident five years ago."

*

Will drove back to the police station in the late afternoon. There was an email waiting for him from Alan Sidebottom's doctor in Cambridge—a reply to a query about the digoxin prescription. The doctor was able to confirm through the pharmacist that Alan Sidebottom had filled the prescription just before leaving England. By the pharmacist's count, there should be somewhere between twenty-six to thirty pills remaining in the prescription, based on the past usage. Twenty-nine pills were found in the digoxin bottle. That meant Professor Sidebottom had not overdosed with his own pills. This was not a suicide, accidental or otherwise.

Will shared the information with Chief Val right away.

"All right," she said. "Now we know we're looking at homicide, she said soberly. Professor Alan Sidebottom was poisoned by an overdose of digitalis—but not by his own hand. The fatal dose did not come from his personal prescription. So, how did somebody get all that digitalis into our guy?"

"Will," she continued. "See if the coroner checked for injection marks. And also, find out if there's another medication that mimics digitalis? And find out how many people at the college are prescribed digoxin."

"Will do," he replied, scribbling down notes. "Do you think someone could have forced pills into Sidebottom, and counted on the fact that nobody would suspect anything other than an accidental overdose? If he was known to be a heavy drinker, maybe the killer counted on Sidebottom being drunk, thinking his death would be chalked up to his own addle-brained, drunken mistake. "

"May be. Except for the fact that there were no defensive marks—no sign of any kind of struggle," the Chief said.

"Maybe in his state of inebriation he wouldn't have been able to put up much of a fight," Will said.

"Yeah, it's possible all right. According to your report it looks like there's no shortage of motives. But, if there was someone there with him, forcing the digoxin into him somehow—wouldn't there have been *some* indication of a struggle? Nothing was disturbed in the cottage; nothing was out of place. Nothing was knocked onto the floor or overturned." Chief Val reached for her mug of coffee, looking back down at the open folder in front of her. "The professor was clean, nothing under the fingernails, no scratches or bruises or suspicious marks."

"Did the results come back on the stomach contents?" Will said. "Maybe the digitalis was administered in food."

"Not yet. I'll let you know as soon as I get the report," the Chief said.

"One other thing," said Will.

"An instructor I interviewed at the college remembers something Professor Sidebottom said right before he ran off that night. It doesn't make any kind of sense, but I'm working on it."

"What was it?" asked the Chief.

"'Time for the Barnet Fair hat-toss'", Will read from his notes.

Chief Val stared at him blankly.

"I told you it didn't make sense," Will shrugged. "I'm working on it."

When Will returned to his office he checked his messages. There was one from Edwina. He returned the call and she answered right away.

"Can you meet me somewhere?" Edwina said breathlessly.

"What's going on?" Will asked.

"I think I've got something for you," she replied. "I don't want to talk about it on the phone, or in my office, for that matter. Can I come over to the police station?"

"Sure—"

"I'll be there in ten minutes."

Chapter 8

Edwina locked up her bike outside the New Guilford Police Station, a low, brick building with American and state flags flying in front. A cement walkway bordered by uneven shrubs led to the main entrance.

Edwina asked at the Information Desk for Detective Tenney. The woman at the front desk was dressed too young for her age, which looked to be late thirties. Her ruched purple blouse looked a size too small, and her oversized hoop earrings looked dangerously heavy. She regarded Edwina coolly.

"In reference to what?"

"He's expecting me," Edwina said impatiently.

"Name?"

"Edwina Goodman."

The woman dialed an extension on the phone.

"Will, there is a Miss Goodman here who wishes to speak with you," she said into the phone, looking anywhere but at Edwina.

Hanging up the phone, she spoke in a deflated tone.

"Turn right when you get to the hallway, second door on your left,"

Will stood outside his office door, waiting to greet Edwina.

"Hi," he said. "Please come in."

Edwina sat down, a little out of breath. She sat leaning forward in the chair at a slightly awkward angle.

"Would you like to take off your backpack?" Will asked. "You might be more comfortable."

Edwina removed her backpack and set it down on the floor beside her. She removed a bottle of water from it and took a swig.

"I did a little research," she began, shoving her bangs aside.

"Once I remembered that bizarre phrase Professor Sidebottom muttered when he ran away, I got to thinking." Edwina's eyes glinted with excitement.

"Time I got the Barnet Fair hat toss," she repeated slowly. "Only it wasn't 'hat toss'—it was 'hack toff'. It suddenly came to me! 'Toff' is British slang, meaning an upper class person. So that got me thinking that maybe the whole phrase was British slang."

Will listened intently.

"I found some books in the main library that confirmed my suspicions," she continued excitedly. "Turns out 'Barnet Fair' is slang for 'hair'."

Will looked at her with a confused expression. Edwina had seen the same expression often enough in her classroom.

"It's called rhyming slang. It's an English thing—like—'white cliffs of Dover' means, 'hangover'," she explained. "Or—'apples and pears' means stairs."

Edwina paused a beat to allow Will to process this information.

"Time—I—got—the—Barnet—Fair—hack—toff," she said slowly. "Substitute the word 'hair' for 'Barnet Fair' and say it," she said.

"Time—I—got—the—hair—hack—toff," Will repeated.

"You see?" Edwina exclaimed. "Time I got the hair hacked off! Time to get a haircut! What if Professor Sidebottom went to get a haircut after I had dinner with him? What if something happened during the haircut that freaked him out? Maybe he ran into someone who gave him a scare—maybe someone from his past, an old nemesis or something—and the shock caused him to have a heart attack?"

Will nodded and started to say something, but in her excitement Edwina interrupted him.

"There are five hair places in New Guilford," she continued. "I've already checked. Three hair salons for women, one barbershop and one unisex place."

"Please don't tell me you went to all of them and asked about Professor Sidebottom," Will interjected.

"Of course I did!" Edwina replied. "I had to go where my research—"

"There's something you don't know," he interrupted, "and if you'd just listen to me for a second . . ."

They glared at each other for a few uncomfortable seconds.

"There has been a development in Professor Sidebottom's death," Will said. "It is now a murder investigation."

He let these words sink in slowly.

"Professor Sidebottom died of a massive heart attack—caused by digitalis poisoning," Will continued. "Which means that it's dangerous for you to go around, randomly asking people all kinds of questions. Having said that, I *would* appreciate it if you shared with me what you found out when you canvassed the hair salons and barber shops."

"Murder?" Edwina said, a few beats behind.

"Yes. Professor Sidebottom was intentionally killed by person or persons unknown. Now, about your interviews."

"Jesus, murder!" Edwina repeated. "The hair salons? I completely struck out. Nobody admitted to seeing the professor, or cutting his hair, or anything. Someone must be lying."

"Well, we'll see about that. I'll find out in due course," Will said. "By the way, that was a pretty good piece of detective work you did, figuring out that British slang stuff," Will said. "Listen, thanks for coming in to see me. I really appreciate it."

Edwina did not move from the chair. She looked at Will expectantly. "So, what's next?" she said.

"Well," he began, "I imagine you'll be getting back to the college. I'm sure you have a class to teach, or papers to grade. As for me, I'll be getting along with the investigation. You've really been a big help."

Edwina thought Will was being plain rude. Now that she knew Professor Sidebottom's death was a murder, her curiosity was full blown. She couldn't possibly step aside from the investigation now. After all, hadn't she been the one who dug up the first significant clue in the case—the haircut business?

Will stood up, signaling for Edwina to do the same.

"How about if we stay in touch, and I let you know how things are progressing?" he said solicitously. "I really don't want you out there conducting your own, private investigation. It could be dangerous. Don't forget that curiosity killed the cat!"

How very patronizing, Edwina thought. *Lucky for me cats have nine lives.*

*

Edwina returned to Sanborn House and knocked on Professor Cake's door.

"Come," came Prof. Cake's thin voice.

"Ah, Edwina," she smiled. "I've been expecting you."

"Why is that?" Edwina asked, settling into her usual chair.

"Because you feel you are somehow responsible for Alan Sidebottom's death—even though you are not—and you don't know what to do about it."

"Well?" Edwina replied.

"Well, what?" the old lady said.

"What *should* I do about it? I can't help thinking that if I had stayed longer with Professor Sidebottom the night he died, everything might have been different," Edwina said. "I could have protected him."

"Edwina, my dear, you must know that whoever wanted Alan dead was going to kill him sooner or later."

"How did you know it was murder?" Edwina asked.

"Just a hunch. Which you've now confirmed for me," Professor Cake replied. "Do you really believe you could have prevented it?"

Edwina looked at her lap for an answer.

"No. I suppose not," Edwina replied. "My problem is, it happened on my watch. So I can't help feeling somehow responsible."

Professor Cake leaned her head back against the chair and closed her eyes. A few moments passed in silence, and Edwina wondered if she had dozed off.

"So, you are wanting to approach this problem as a mathematical proof?" Professor Cake asked, fixing Edwina with a level gaze.

"Nobody's opinion will help you feel better? You won't settle for anything less than *quod erat demonstrandum*?" the old professor continued.

Edwina nodded again.

"Then let me ask you something," Professor Cake said. "Remember that night at the New World, when Helen had too much to drink, and confessed to all of us about a youthful affair with Alan?"

Edwina nodded.

"Consider that fact more carefully. See how many variations you come up with by studying that bit of data. You may be pleasantly surprised by what you find. I think it's an important piece of the puzzle."

"And by the way," the old professor added, "that handsome, young detective who has been spending time around here has a wee crush on you, in case you're interested in such things."

Excited about this new angle on the investigation, Edwina started back down the hallway toward her own office where she would be able to shut the door and think about it to her heart's content.

Donald Gaylord came scurrying toward her halfway down the hall.

"Edwina, they're saying Alan Sidebottom was murdered! Is it true?" he said anxiously.

Wow, word sure travels fast! Edwina thought.

"I think so, yes," she said.

"My god! Who would do such a thing?" Donald gasped. "It's unthinkable! I simply can't believe it!"

"It's awful, I know," Edwina said. "Are you okay, Don? You look a little flushed."

"No, no; I'm fine," he answered. "Murder! It's such a shock. Do you think someone in the Department could be responsible?"

Before Edwina could answer, Donald turned away abruptly.

"Must dash, I'm late!" he called back, bounding down the hall.

Edwina stood there for a moment, wondering why Donald would be in such a nervous state. Against her better judgment she decided to follow him back to his office and do a little reconnaissance, having no idea what she would do once there.

When she reached Donald's office the door was closed but she could hear his voice from inside. Pauses in the conversation and the absence of a second voice told her Donald was on the phone. As a subterfuge she took her phone out of her pocket and pretended to be having a text conversation. If someone came along she would continue the ruse and slowly stroll away, still 'texting'. In the meantime, she eavesdropped on Donald's conversation.

The pitch of his voice was subdued but sounded angry, then he would backtrack to sounding apologetic and contrite, and back to angry again. Edwina managed to catch only a few words here and there. The last word she could make out before the conversation ended was "weekend". Edwina wondered if Donald were speaking to his wife. When the phone call ended she walked quickly back down the hallway.

Edwina stopped in Reception and poured a cup of coffee, adding milk and sugar. She returned to her office and closed the door. Setting the coffee down carefully on her cluttered desk, she sat down and closed her eyes.

She tried to imagine a set of facts that would illuminate Donald's nervous behavior in the hallway, and his alternately angry and beseeching tone of voice on the phone call. Did he suspect his own wife of somehow being involved with Alan Sidebottom's murder? Or did he think she might suspect him? How would Donald's wife fit into an equation? Edwina wondered if she would recognize Donald's wife if she were to see her, having never met her, and knowing her only from the picture on Donald's desk. Had Edwina possibly seen her around town in recent days, and not known it?

Edwina opened her eyes and took a sip of hot, sweet coffee. Her thoughts drifted back to the conversation with Nedda Cake.

How many variations of the data are there? Edwina repeated in her mind.

Helen Mann and Alan Sidebottom had an affair some thirty years ago. Could this information be damaging? And if it was somehow a threat to someone, are we talking about blackmail? But why would Helen confess to a long-ago affair if it might do damage to her or someone else? Maybe Helen didn't mean to blurt it out at all—maybe she doesn't even remember saying it— after all, she was drunk at the time.

Edwina gazed out the window, sipping the comfortingly milky-sweet coffee.

Wait a minute, she thought. *What if their liaison wasn't so long ago? What if Helen and Alan Sidebottom had kept on seeing each other all these years? Could Alan be the reason Helen never married? Did Alan come to Cushing to end their affair? Did Helen kill him in some sort of apoplectic fit of scorn and rage?*

The view outside Edwina's office window was always active. The continual motion and flow of life helped her think, aided in her momentum of thought. Members of the college population came and went along the path—on foot, on bikes—crisscrossing the Green in all directions. Hawks glided and swooped over the hills in the distance. Squirrels chased each other up and down the trees and across the Green.

Directly below Edwina's window a young mother was pushing a sleeping toddler in a stroller, a sippy cup clutched in her little hand.

Something suddenly clicked in Edwina's mind.

Helen and Alan had an affair thirty years ago.

What if a child resulted?

*

Will visited 'Eazy Cutz' bright and early, the first on his list of New Guilford's hair cutting establishments. The owner was a personable man named Tony, who offered to give the detective a free trim during the interview, which he politely declined. Tony's manner was open and friendly, and he had photographs of his grandchildren taped around the edges of the wall-sized mirror. Tony did not recognize the photograph Will showed him of Alan Sidebottom.

The owner of Total Allure assured Will her clients were all women. No exceptions.

"No offense," the owner explained good-naturedly, "but that's part of the appeal of spending a couple of hours at the salon. No men! Most women don't want men around when their heads are wrapped in tin foil and they reek of chemicals," she laughed.

Next on his list was the lone barbershop in town. The owner, an elderly man with thinning hair dyed black, smelled strongly of cologne. He was giving a customer a shave when Will entered the shop.

The tiny establishment reminded Will of childhood trips to the barbershop. While his dad got a shave and a haircut, young William Tenney watched intently, sucking on a lollipop and keeping a sharp eye on the razor-wielding barber, making sure no harm would come to his dad.

The barber had no recollection of Alan Sidebottom.

Leah's Place was next. The newest of the five hair-care establishments, Leah's salon was located in a white washed brick building in a little alleyway. Whiskey barrel planters blazed with brightly colored chrysanthemums in front of the shops. Leah, tall and slender with dark hair, looked to be in her thirties. She greeted Will cordially. He showed her the photograph of Alan Sidebottom.

"Oh yes, I remember him," she said. "I let him in the shop for a haircut one night when I was just about to close up," she said pleasantly. "Poor man seemed desperate for a hair cut, and also a little bit drunk. I felt sorry for him, I guess."

"Did you know he was found dead the following morning?" Will inquired.

"Yes, I heard it on the news," Leah said. "So awful. What happened to him?"

"A heart attack."

"Oh, poor man!" she gasped.

"Was there much conversation when he was here?" asked Will.

"Well," Leah said, cocking her head to one side and searching the ceiling, "just the usual sort of stuff. I asked him where he was from, how he liked New Guilford, if he had kids—that kind of thing. He wasn't very chatty. I think he might have even dozed off for a few minutes at the sink."

"How long would you say he was here?"

"Uh, well, let's see. First we were at the sink. I washed his hair, I conditioned it, and I probably de-mineralized it, because it was in pretty bad shape. Very dried out, and a lot of breakage. Then he came over to the chair, and I gave him a haircut and a comb out. So, altogether, he was probably here for about thirty-five minutes."

"Comb out?" the detective echoed.

"I blow-dried his hair and styled it," she said agreeably.

"Did he say anything when he left?"

"Nothing in particular. Just 'thanks' and 'good-night', and that's really it," Leah said.

"Did he mention anything about where he was going, when he left?"

"No, I don't think so. I just assumed he was going home."

"How did he pay?"

"He had one of my flyers for a fifty percent discount. The rest he paid in cash. I remember, because he gave me a big tip."

"Well, thank-you for your help," Will said, placing his card on her desk. "If you think of anything else – anything at all—please call me."

*

Edwina stopped in Reception to check her mailbox, something she avoided doing with any regularity. It was stuffed full. She carried the pile of mail back to her office and dumped it on her desk, and began sorting through the coupons, catalogs, flyers, and envelopes.

She set aside a sporting catalog, the new issue of *Canoe & Kayak Magazine,* and a paycheck, and was about to toss out the rest when she noticed a flyer advertising 50 % off the first haircut at 'Leah's Place'. Edwina stared at it.

She jogged down the hall to Reception. Ruth Benjamin was at her desk, typing.

"Ruth? Quick question," Edwina said, holding up the pink flyer. "Did everybody in the department get one of these?"

"Yup. There was a pile of those sitting on my desk, so I stuck one in everybody's box. Why?"

"Oh, nothing, I was just curious. Thanks," Edwina said.

Edwina sat at her desk and stared out the window, wondering about the significance, if any, of the advertisement for a hair salon. She opened a desk drawer and fished around until she came up with the card Will had given her.

She picked up her phone and texted him.

I hope I'm not being a Bossy Boots, but our whole department got flyers for a discount haircut at Leah's Place in town. Thought you should check it out asap. Maybe Sidebottom went there.

*

Will read Edwina's text as he walked through the parking lot of the police station. He climbed into an old Ford pick-up truck, sat behind the wheel and texted her back.

Good work, BB. Sidebottom got a haircut at Leah's sure enough.

He drove through downtown Old Guilford, through its quiet residential streets, and into the surrounding hills toward the neighboring town of Westover. Halfway to Westover he turned onto a rural route for a few miles, and then onto a steep, dirt road through dense woods. He parked on a remote property with his half-built house, his tipi out back, and a spring-fed pond, mostly hidden by foliage.

The plans for the house were laid out on a makeshift table—a wooden door set across two sawhorses—in the kitchen area of the house. Will poured a large container of clam chowder into a saucepan and heated it on a double-burner hot plate. He studied the plans while he ate, making notations in pencil here and there.

What would eventually be the living room area of the house was currently fashioned into a workspace. Will changed into a pair of jeans and a sweatshirt, grabbed a cedar board and ran it through the miter saw, cutting it to size for clapboarding. He repeated this until twenty new clapboards had been added to the pile.

Although plumbing lines had been run before the concrete foundation was poured, the bathtub and shower would not be installed for another few weeks, at least. When he was finished working Will trotted out to the pond and stripped down in full view of the neighboring wildlife.

The last rays of evening sun made the treetops appear incandescent He bathed quickly in the cold water, and changed into a pair of clean sweatpants and tee shirt. Before retiring to the tipi with a Louis L'Amour book, Will swept the sawdust around the miter saw into a neat pile, scooped it up with a dust pan, and dumped it into a half-filled trash bag. He used water from a plastic jug to rinse out his dinner dishes, dried them off, and trudged up the hill at the back of the house.

The tipi's interior was surprisingly spacious. Will had studied *The Indian Tipi: Its History, Construction, and Use*, by Gladys and Reginald Laubin (published 1957). He had finally mastered adjusting the smoke flaps, so the smoke could get out but the rain would not get in. Seventeen twenty-seven foot poles around the perimeter held the tipi in place. Camping lanterns lit the inside, which was scattered with tools, books, and clothes. The bed, a sleeping bag on a raised cot, was perfectly sufficient for the duration.

Will lay in bed gazing up at the peak of the tipi. Listening to the owls and bullfrogs in the background, he thought about the case. Of course, there were still Department members he had yet to interview, and he could not speculate about them.

Donald Gaylord had distinguished himself by his willingness to point the finger in so many different directions without a moment's hesitation, and by getting Will's hackles up in record time. Donald struck Will as untrustworthy, the way he had tried to duck questions and control the interview. Donald Gaylord was hiding something.

Charlotte Cadell had been more forthcoming, but Will thought she, too, was withholding information.

There was something more than a broken engagement that made Charlotte so prematurely spinsterish. Charlotte was an attractive woman. Will wanted to know why her disappointment of years ago had destroyed her confidence—or faith, or something—so completely.

And Helen Mann. Her history with Alan Sidebottom included an affair, and goodness knew what else. Will tried to imagine Helen as a younger, attractive woman, but he was getting sleepy. His thoughts were growing hazy, and his imagination fell short.

He forced himself up one last time to stoke the fire in the wood-burning stove. The nights were getting cold up on the mountain. He added logs to the fire and stirred the coals. The sweet aroma of wood smoke settled around him like a soft blanket as he scrunched down into the sleeping bag. Edwina Goodman popped into his mind, with her glinting hazel eyes and pale freckles.

A few minutes later Will was dead to the world.

Chapter 9

There was frost on the ground Saturday morning. Edwina sat at the kitchen table dressed in a fleece vest zipped up over her nightgown, with a steaming pot of tea.

A computer search quickly resulted in information about the Brussels conference where Helen and Alan had had their fling thirty-five years earlier. A child resulting from their affair would be in his or her mid-thirties.

Edwina began a new search.

Starting with department members Seth Dubin, Lois Lieberman, and secretary Ruth Benjamin—all of who were around their mid-thirties—she started looking up birth records. As there were a number of people in and around the department who were the right age to be the child of Helen and Alan, it proved to be a time-consuming effort, and after an hour and a half Edwina had come up with nothing useful.

Hunger demanding her attention, Edwina made breakfast. She sat in the wicker rocking chair with a plate of eggs and toast, and watched the birds and squirrels outside the kitchen window. The squirrels were busy burying acorns for the winter months ahead. The birds seemed to be enjoying the day as they chatted across the bird feeder and ignored the squirrels, which darted back and forth feverishly, flicking their tails nervously as if the world were coming to an end.

Edwina sopped up the last bit of egg yolk with a piece of toast and washed it down with tea.

While she washed the breakfast dishes a thought came to her, another name to search, someone else in the right age category to be the child of Alan Sidebottom and Helen Mann. Edwina dried her hands quickly and sat down at the computer.

She found Sheila Dubin's maiden name listed in a biographical entry about Seth on a scientific web site. Now she could search for Sheila's birth record.

Edwina could find no birth record for Sheila Dubin, nee Donovan. That could mean that Sheila had a different last name when she was born, and that the Donovans were not her birth parents. What if Helen Mann and Alan Sidebottom turned out to be Sheila's birth parents, and had given her up for adoption? Did Sheila know it? Was it mere coincidence that Sheila had married a physicist and ended up at Cushing?

What if Sheila didn't know Helen and Alan were her birth parents? What if she unwittingly killed her own father in an act of revenge for humiliating Seth and ruining his chances for advancement?

Then another thought occurred to her.

She kept thinking about the night she overheard Donald Gaylord with a woman in his office at Sanborn House. She was just about positive it was Sheila Dubin. What if Donald found out Sheila killed Professor Sidebottom, in a rage after his cruel treatment at the party toward Seth? Could Sheila have possibly involved Donald in her crazy bid for revenge? She was pushy enough to talk him into it! Edwina could never figure out why kind and gentle Seth Dubin had married such an aggressive woman as Sheila in the first place.

Edwina looked at the clock. It was almost lunchtime.

She called Will to share these latest ideas.

"Where are you?" he asked.

"At home. Why?"

"I'm in town today—doing laundry at the Laundromat. My usual Saturday routine. Why don't I stop by your house on my way home? I'm just about finished here."

Edwina looked down at her nightgown.

"Sure. How about half an hour? It's number thirty-eight, Canaan Farm Road."

Edwina trotted upstairs, showered and dressed. She made the bed, tidied up the house, and made a pot of tea.

*

Will was prompt. Edwina showed him into the kitchen.

"Great stove," he said. "It's a classic model, did you know that? It's a shame they stopped making this one. I don't know why they discontinued it. How's it heat for you?"

"Great. Heats the whole house."

"I see you burn ash," he said, remarking on the basket full of split logs. "I've got a couple cords of oak that burns as well as the ash, and it has a nice, sweet smell to it. I could drop some off for you, if you like."

Edwina was surprised by the unexpected offer.

"Oh, really? That'd be great," she said.

A pot of tea was warming on the woodstove. Edwina filled two mugs with steaming, black tea and set them on the table, alongside a small pitcher of milk, a jar of local honey, and spoons.

"Nice house," Will said, taking a sip of tea.

"Looks like you get a lot of customers," he added, watching the steady activity at the bird feeder.

Edwina laughed.

"Yeah, they practically eat me out of house and home, the swine," she said.

"So what's up?" Will said.

Edwina leaned forward on her elbows, her hands overlapped on the kitchen table.

"I don't know if this will have any great bearing on the case," she began, "but I have some information about the department I thought you should know."

Edwina's stomach growled. She took a sip of tea to quiet it.

"I have reason to think that Seth Dubin's wife, Sheila, may be having an affair with Donald Gaylord," she said. "I was working late one night at Sanborn House. I thought I was the only person in the building, but then I heard voices coming from another office. I'm pretty sure it was Donald and Sheila Dubin. And this was in the middle of the night."

Will sipped his tea.

"Let me make sure I follow so far," he said. "You spent the night on college property, spying on members of the department."

"I did spend the night in Sanborn House, yes, but I spent the night there working, and the eavesdropping thing was sort of an accident," Edwina answered defensively.

"Go on."

"Sheila wears a very distinctive perfume. It's really pretty overbearing. I smelled it the night of the party for Professor Sidebottom. When I was in Donald's office a couple days ago, I'm just about positive I smelled it. I think it's possible that Sheila was so enraged at Professor Sidebottom because of the way he treated her husband, Seth, at the party that night, that she killed him."

Will listened.

"And it's possible that Sheila got Donald Gaylord involved, somehow. Or if he's not directly involved, I'll bet he knows she did it."

Edwina regarded Will in earnest, her wide eyes focused intently. The edges of her ears poked out through her hair, still damp from the shower. The perfumed scent of shampoo mingled agreeably with the smell of wood smoke.

"What do you think?" she said.

"It's certainly an interesting thought," Will said.

"Donald Gaylord was so eager to point the finger of suspicion toward anybody else, he's got to be hiding something.   I agree Sheila Dubin has motive—although not the strongest motive—payback for the public humiliation of her husband on the night of the party. She sees Professor Sidebottom's behavior as a serious setback to her husband's career."

Edwina's stomach growled loudly again.

Will got up from the table and walked to the refrigerator.

"Let me see here. How about a grilled cheese and tomato sandwich?" he said.

Edwina watched while he buttered the bread, sliced cheese and tomatoes, and cooked the sandwiches to gooey perfection in a skillet on top of the woodstove. He set them on the table and rinsed the cutting board and knife, leaving them in the dish drainer. He wrapped up the remaining ingredients and put them back in the fridge.

"Do you consider Seth Dubin a suspect?" Edwina said biting into a warm mouthful of sandwich, blissfully unaware of the long string of melted cheese dangling from the corner of her mouth.

Will re-filled their mugs with hot, black tea.

"I never liked him much for the murder. He's still a possible, though. Everybody is, for now," he said, handing Edwina a napkin.

Chapter 10

Paolo and Francesca Rossetti invited Lois Lieberman and Ravi Kapoor for dinner on the weekend.

Of the three colleagues only Paolo, a transplant from Rome, was married. His wife, Francesca, also from Rome, pregnant with their first child, taught Italian language and literature at the college. The Rossettis lived in a spacious Victorian house near campus that was divided into two apartments, one on the first floor and one on the second. They resided on the ground floor. Compared with their compact apartment in Trastevere, the New Guilford digs felt lavish. Paolo, a keen gardener, grew vegetables and flowers at the back of the house.

Lois and Ravi were over for dinner. Both Paolo and Francesca enjoyed cooking and sharing their table with friends. Lois arrived with a bottle of wine in hand, and Ravi brought flowers for Francesca.

"How are you feeling?" Lois asked Francesca.

"Fat! Actually, I feel great—just a little tired," she said.

"You are not fat—you are more beautiful than ever!" Paolo exclaimed, handing glasses of bubbly *moscato* to Lois and Ravi.

"What's going on with the investigation?" Francesca asked, sipping sparkling water and stirring a pot of risotto.

"Paolo and I can't help wondering if Mitchell Fender might be involved, but I think Lois has other ideas," Ravi said.

"Oh?" said Francesca.

"I'm not saying she did it," Lois said, "but if you had seen her reaction when Alan Sidebottom made fun of Seth at the cocktail party . . ."

"We're talking about Sheila Dubin, I take it?" Francesca said.

"I'm telling you," Lois said, "the look she gave Sidebottom was pure venom. Total hatred. I wouldn't put it past her."

"Still, it's a long way to go from being pissed off at somebody, to committing murder," Paolo said.

"The few times I've met Sheila Dubin," Francesca said, "I could almost believe she has it in her. There's something unpleasant about her . . ."

"What about Mitch Fender?" Paolo said. "He has the perfect motive. Everybody knows that Alan Sidebottom was an intellectual pirate—he took ideas wherever he liked—he robbed poor Mitch blind. The poor guy probably snapped."

"The sad part of it is, I don't think Mitchell would have snapped if his wife hadn't left him," said Ravi. "In a million years, I don't believe Mitchell would go off the deep end if she hadn't moved out. It must have been the last straw." He sipped *moscato*. "Is there anybody else, anybody we're not thinking of?"

"What about Seth, himself?" said Paolo.

"Don't be ridiculous!" snapped Lois. "Seth wouldn't hurt the proverbial fly!"

"Even *I* know that's a preposterous idea!" Francesca agreed. "Seth Dubin? *Impossibile!*"

"I don't know—" Paolo speculated. "Maybe when you are that gentle and docile, you eventually explode.

Maybe things build up inside you for so long, and then––kaboom!"

"No, I can't see it, not Seth! More likely, one of us!" laughed Ravi.

Paolo dressed and mixed the salad, and set it on the dining room table, alongside a large bowl of risotto, a loaf of Italian bread, plates and utensils. Francesca brought over glasses and a bottle of wine from the kitchen.

"*Alla tavola!*" she said.

"Oh, wow. This is delicious," said Lois, tasting a bite of risotto.

"Mm, fantastic!" agreed Ravi.

"What about the two of them colluding – what about Mitchell Fender and Sheila Dubin in it together?" Francesca said, serving the salad. "Mitchell Fender and Sheila Dubin—getting together to kill Alan Sidebottom. Maybe when they realized that each had a motive they decided to pool their resources?"

Paolo tore off a piece of bread.

"Mitch Fender and Sheila Dubin plotting together? Highly improbable! Can you really see the two of them colluding? They would more likely end up killing each other," Paolo laughed.

Lois Lieberman took a sip of wine and shook her head.

"How Seth ended up with a she-animal like Sheila is a mystery to me."

Francesca threw Paolo a look. He caught it.

They had coffee and Italian cornmeal cake in the living room. Ravi and Paolo played a game of chess. Francesca and Lois chatted on the sofa.

"Are you coming hiking with us tomorrow?" Lois asked.

Francesca patted her protruding belly.

"Oh, sure," she said. "I have a while to go, yet, and my doc says the walking is good for me and for the baby."

A text message rang on Lois's phone.

"Sorry," Lois said. "I need to check this." Lois read the message and texted something back. She rose to leave.

"Sorry, guys. I've got to get going. I said I might meet somebody later. Thanks for dinner, Francesca. It was absolutely delicious. See you this weekend. 'Night, guys, see you at work tomorrow."

 Francesca walked Lois to the door and they hugged good night. She looked at Paolo and Ravi with a puzzled expression.

"Is she dating anyone?" Francesca said.

"Beats me," Paolo said, moving a pawn.

Ravi shrugged.

"Well, I can tell you pretty definitely that she *is*," Francesca said. "Lois's cheeks turned bright pink when she read that text."

"Wait a minute," Paolo said, looking up from the game. "Now that I think of it, there was something funny that happened the night Ravi and I were at the lab—remember, Ravi, the night Lois didn't show up?"

Ravi looked up from the chessboard.

"You remember," Paolo repeated. "She texted you about having stomach 'flu."

"Oh, yes, right. I remember now," Ravi said, turning his attention back to the game board. "What's your point?"

"After I left the lab, I picked up a few things for Lois—crackers and ginger ale—and I left them by her front door," Paolo said.

"As I was leaving her house I saw—or I *thought* I saw—a curtain moving in an upstairs window. Now

I'm wondering if Lois had company that night? Maybe she wasn't really sick?" Paolo said.

"Well, good for her," Ravi replied without looking up. "She's a great girl. I just hope the guy is good enough for her."

"By the way, Ravi," Francesca said. "I always wondered why *you* never asked Lois out? Paolo and I have met some of the women you date, and Lois would make a nice change," she said teasingly.

Ravi stayed focused on the chessboard.

"Not really my type," he said, moving a bishop. "I quite like Charlotte Cadell, though. I was thinking of asking her to dinner some night."

Chapter 11

Will paid another visit to the Carriage House cottage where Professor Sidebottom had stayed during his short time in New Guilford, and where he had died. Perhaps something had been overlooked.

He parked his car in one of the campus lots, and walked along the footpath that eventually snaked its way around to the Carriage House.

Charlotte Cadell peered from a window in Sanborn House at Will. She craned her neck in order to see him until he finally passed out of her sight. She sat at her desk with an uneasy feeling, unable to concentrate on her work. She hoped the police would clear things up quickly. It was awfully unsettling having had a murder take place practically next door to where she worked.

*

There had been no evidence of a break-in when Will and his officers first examined the scene at the Carriage House. The doors and windows were locked. Alan Sidebottom could easily have let his killer in through either the front door, or the rear service door at the kitchen. And since Professor Sidebottom had been drunk at the time, he might have let in anyone, even someone he did not know. Comings and goings at the Carriage House were very difficult to observe by passers-by, set back and obscured from the path as it was by trees and foliage. No witnesses had come forth.

The Carriage House and environs were restricted by yellow police tape. Will ducked into the cordoned area and let himself into the cottage with a key. He stood in the center of the living room and closed his eyes, as if hoping to absorb new information about the crime through osmosis or inspiration. After a few minutes, he walked into the bedroom. Alan's lifeless body had been discovered in the morning, under the covers in bed, dressed in pajamas. He had died in his sleep from a heart attack.

Will sat down at the dressing table in the corner of the bedroom, and slowly gazed around the room. Diffuse light filtered indirectly through sheer curtains, reflecting off the glossy pale blue walls.

There had been no cup or glass by the bedside that might have revealed traces of a fatal dose of digitalis. Still, someone could have forced a fatal concoction on Alan, rinsed the glass afterward, exited the cottage through a window, and closed it behind them. Every glass, cup, and utensil had been tested for fingerprints, as had the entire place. The cottage and grounds had been gone over meticulously for every manner of evidence, but the place was clean.

How had the fatal dose of digitalis been administered? Alan's body had been checked for injection marks, and none were found. Food was the likely possibility. The results from tests being done on the stomach contents were not back, yet.

Will sat down on the bare mattress, the bedding having been stripped. There was a faint odor in the room, difficult to identify. He leaned over toward the night table and put his nose next to the wood, touching it. Was it a wood wax or polishing product he smelled? The scent got fainter when he sniffed the wood table. The odor was unfamiliar – slightly chemical, but also sweetly pungent. Will walked through the rooms of the cottage, stopping to smell the curtains, the carpet, inside the drawers and closets, the furniture cushions. He returned to the bedroom and sat down again on the bed. The scent seemed to be strongest there in the bedroom. He walked slowly around the bedroom again. The smell got fainter. It was strongest near the mattress. Will sat down and scratched his head.

A crime scene where the only evidence is an illusive scent!

Will locked the cottage door and walked to Sanborn House. He headed up to the second floor, and knocked on Dr. Seth Dubin's door.

A slight man in his thirties with sandy hair and horn-rimmed glasses, Seth Dubin had a gentle and kindly air about him. When he spoke it was in a soft-spoken voice.

Will introduced himself and showed Seth identification.

"I understand Professor Sidebottom was something of a hero of yours?"

"Oh, yes," Seth replied. "Very much so. I was thrilled when he came to Cushing. Honestly, I could hardly believe my good fortune."

"But I also understand that he was less than friendly when you finally met him at the cocktail reception?"

"Oh, I expect he had had too much to drink," Seth replied, folding his hands in his lap.

"Might there be some other reason Professor Sidebottom was so disagreeable toward you? A personal reason?"

"I really have no idea," Seth smiled. "But my guess would be, he behaved like a bully because he was used to behaving that way. And because he could get away with it. It didn't particularly bother me. I attached no real meaning to it. I've seen other successful people behave like bullies.   Perhaps it's an occupational hazard."

"What occupation are we talking about?"

A weary smile crept over Seth Dubin's face.

"The occupation of having power over other people, I guess you could say," Seth replied.

"Had you ever met Professor Sidebottom before he arrived at Cushing?"

"Never met him, no," Seth said.   "Of course, everyone in the field is highly aware of him."

"Was your wife acquainted with Professor Sidebottom? I understand she was also at the cocktail party," Will said.

"My wife?"

"Yes, sir.   I believe she accompanied you to the reception for Professor Sidebottom Friday evening. I wondered if she knew him?"

"Oh, no.   Sheila and I were both meeting Alan Sidebottom for the first time," Seth said.

"My wife enjoys Department functions," Seth continued. "Gives her a chance to get out and socialize, and get to know my colleagues. I think she wishes we had more of a social life."

Will made notes.

"What is your field of special interest, Dr. Dubin?"

"I teach a few beginning courses, for my sins. But my area of research is string theory."

"Similar to Professor Sidebottom's interests?"

"Oh, yes, very much so.   Which is why I was so looking forward to his being at Cushing this semester. There's a lot of very exciting work going on right now, and it would have been fantastic to be able to discuss all of it with Alan Sidebottom. "

Will asked for Seth's account of the gathering at the New World Tavern the evening of Professor Sidebottom's death.   Seth's memories were consistent with the stories of others, and he more or less repeated what Will had already heard.

Will gazed around the office as he got up to leave. There was an advertising flyer sitting on top of a stack of mail, the same pink color as the flyer he had seen in Helen Mann's office. He reached in to retrieve it. It was a copy of the same advertisement for a discounted haircut.

"Where did you get this, Dr. Dubin?"

"That? Oh, those were stuffed into everybody's mailbox, I believe. You could check with Ruth Benjamin, the department secretary."

"Thank-you for your time, Dr. Dubin. If you think of anything, please give me a call."

Seth Dubin presents a very convincing picture of the mild-mannered, gentleman scholar, Will thought as he left Seth's office. *But can anyone really have that much equanimity? He sure takes a lot in his stride. . .*

*

The second floor landing at Sanborn House spilled out into a light and airy reception area. A wall of windows lavished sunlight onto a row of potted geraniums lined up along the sill. Area rugs were scattered throughout the spacious reception area, and low, white bookcases wrapped around the room. Two sofas flanked the fireplace at one end of the room. Department secretary Ruth Benjamin sat at her desk at the other end of the large space.

"Ruth Benjamin? Detective William Tenney from New Guilford P.D.," Will said, proffering identification. "I'd like to ask you some questions, if you have a moment."

Ruth Benjamin looked up and smiled. An appealing woman in her thirties, she was dressed in a cream-colored ruffled blouse and dark skirt.

"Sit down, detective. Can I offer you a cup of coffee?" she asked.

"No thanks. I wanted to ask you about the pink advertisements for a hair salon you distributed into everyone's mailbox, that arrived around the same time Professor Sidebottom came to New Guilford," the detective said.

"Oh, you mean the ones Edwina was asking about?"

"Yes, I expect so," Will replied.

"What did you want to know about them?" Ruth asked.

"If you can remember, when exactly did they arrive, and who delivered them?"

"As a matter of fact, I do remember, because they were sitting on my desk bright and early Monday morning, which was Professor Sidebottom's first day of teaching—and sadly, turned out to be his only day teaching at Cushing. Anyway, the flyers must have been delivered by hand early Monday morning. I usually get here around 8:30, and as I say, they were already here when I arrived, sitting in a nice, neat pile on my desk," Ruth said.

"Did Professor Sidebottom receive his mail on Monday?" he asked.

"Yes, he did. I put his mail on the desk, myself—including the haircut flyer."

"Why did you hand deliver his mail, instead of leaving it the mailroom, along with everyone else's?"

"I thought it would be a nice gesture—you know, a welcoming gesture, for his first day here." Ruth said.

"Did you observe any particular interactions Professor Sidebottom had with anyone in the department? Or anyone at all?"

Ruth thought for a moment before answering.

"It seemed like the whole department was excited about his arrival at Cushing, but other than that . . . well, Professor Mann did stop by my desk a couple of times Monday morning to ask if Professor Sidebottom was looking for her."

Will thanked Ruth Benjamin, and left his card.

*

There was a knock on Edwina's door.

"Come in," she called from her desk.

Seth Dubin walked in and closed the door behind him.

"Got a minute?" he asked.

"Sure thing, sit down."

Seth spoke softly.

"This is somewhat awkward," he began nervously. "I didn't mention it to Detective Tenney, but I think I need to tell someone. It's about Sheila."

"Go ahead", Edwina said quietly.

"It's just that—with Sheila's medical background and training—it crossed my mind that she could have poisoned Professor Sidebottom. She would know exactly how to do it. I know it's a terrible thing to say. But I just can't help thinking it."

"Why would Sheila want to do that?" Edwina asked.

"Well, I don't know if you remember, but the night of the party she was very upset with Professor Sidebottom. He was needling me a bit about my stammer, and Sheila took it very badly. She was furious, as a matter of fact." Seth said. "Just furious."

"Well, has she said anything weird that makes you think she might have actually done it?"

"No. She hasn't said a thing. It's probably just my imagination going crazy," Seth said.

"Yeah, probably. Let's keep it between ourselves for now. No need to broadcast a suspicion. And try not to worry about it, Seth. It's probably just your imagination."

*

A poster was taped to the outside of Mitchell Fender's door, showing a brightly colored biohazard symbol, and printed beneath, 'Biohazard! Infectious Personality!'

The door was ajar, and Will knocked lightly.

"Enter!"

"Dr. Fender? Detective William Tenney from New Guilford P.D. May I have a few moments of your time?"

"Come in, my good man," Mitchell said jovially.

The walls of the cluttered office were covered with colorful posters and signs. Hanging behind Dr. Fender's desk a placard read, "MAY THE m x a BE WITH YOU".

"Dr. Fender we're looking into the death of Alan Sidebottom, which we now know was a murder. To be blunt, Dr. Fender, I understand there was no love lost between you and Professor Sidebottom."

"Unfortunately true," Mitchell Fender said. "Alan Sidebottom was brilliant, but as anyone will tell you he was unscrupulous. He was almost pathological in his disregard for others. I'm sorry to speak ill of the dead––he shouldn't have died—but I have very little good to say about him, regrettably."

Mitchell Fender ran a beefy index finger and thumb over his bushy moustache. Will noticed his fingernails were bitten to the quick.

"I take it you've heard all about the plagiarism incident?"

"Why don't you tell me about it, sir."

"A messy, unfortunate episode. I've been researching the event horizon for many years. For you civilians, this refers to the point of no return—the threshold, the doorway—where matter and energy disappear into the infinite gravitational pull of a black hole. The edge, if you like. Take my word for it, you want to steer clear of these suckers! Very exciting stuff."

Dr. Fender leaned back in the desk chair and stroked his moustache. A pair of red suspenders strained against his ample belly.

"I'm with you, sir, please go on."

With his glasses pushed up on his forehead, Mitchell Fender cradled the back of his head in his interlocked fingers, and rocked gently in the creaking desk chair.

"The long and short of it that Alan Sidebottom— shall we say, 'appropriated'—some of my research and included it in his recent best seller. I pressed charges for theft of intellectual property, but nothing came of it. It couldn't be proved, and the case was dismissed."

"You must have hated Professor Sidebottom for it?"

"You're right; I did. That work would have gotten me tenure, and the respect I . . ."

Dr. Fender's voice faltered, and he fell silent.

"Dr. Fender, sir, I'm told you and Professor Sidebottom were getting along at the Department cocktail reception, laughing together, and so on."

"Life is short, detective," Mitchell said, recovering his composure.

"It's important to seize the day, let bygones be bygones. The deed is done. My colleagues were very supportive of me throughout the whole ordeal, especially Helen Mann, and she's the boss."

"I appreciate your forthrightness, Dr. Fender. Would you mind telling me where you were Monday night, the night Alan Sidebottom died?"

"Let's see, now. Monday night," he said, stroking his moustache. "Righto, got it! I was at home alone, making a pot of stew and watching the football game on television."

"What did you think of the game?" Will asked.

"We've got too many guys out with injuries. But there's still time to come back!" Mitchell Fender said with enthusiasm.

"Thank-you for your time, Dr. Fender. If you think of anything else, please contact me," Will said.

Chapter 12

A typical lunch for Will would be a take-out sandwich from Earl's, eaten at his desk at the police station. But today was different. Since The New World Tavern figured into the investigation, Will decided to have lunch there.

Will had a good view of the whole restaurant from a small table in the corner.   He showed identification to his server and asked if might speak to the owner. Louis Canevari appeared moments later walking briskly toward Will, and looking anxious.

"Good afternoon, sir. What can I do for you? No trouble, I hope?"

"No, nothing like that. Please take a seat," Will said genially.

The diminutive proprietor relaxed visibly and sat down.

"We're investigating a death at the college, and I understand a group of students and faculty from Cushing was here on Tuesday night. From the Physics Department. Were you here Tuesday night?"

Louis Canevari spoke energetically, his words seeming to launch out of him like missiles.

"Yes, I know just who you're `talking about," he said. "Some of them come in here regular. Edwina Goodman—she used to work here—she's a great girl. Comes in here all the time."

"Did you notice anything strange or different about the way any of them were acting—anything you might have overheard, or something like that?" asked Will. "Maybe an altercation or an argument?"

Will was momentarily distracted by the appearance of Seth Dubin, looking uncharacteristically dour, accompanied by an attractive woman wearing a close-fitting outfit.

"I'm sorry, Mr. Canevari. Would you please repeat that?"

"I was just saying – a couple of them stayed behind and kinda' got into a disagreement. A man and a lady."

"Can you describe them, please?" said Will, his attention fully back with Louis Canevari.

"The guy—very nice-looking man, well-dressed, handsome. The woman, she was kinda' mousey—you know what I mean—not bad looking, just needs to fix herself up a little bit. Probably a brainy type. "

"How old would you guess this woman was?"

"I would say they were both around forty, give or take," Louis Canevari said.

Will wondered if Louis Canevari might be describing Donald Gaylord and Charlotte Cadell.

"Did you hear what the argument was about?" Will pressed.

"That, I couldn't tell you. They were very hush-hush. I could tell it was an argument, though. You been married as long as I have, you can spot an argument a mile away!"

"Thank-you, Mr. Canevari. You've been very helpful."

"Enjoy your lunch, sir. I highly recommend the trout. Please, come again, and bring your police friends!"

Will glanced across the room at Seth Dubin and his lunch partner several times. Their conversation looked serious, but they were seated too far away and Will could not overhear any of it. The couple ordered a bottle of wine, and the woman proceeded to drink most of it, only picking at her food. The discussion appeared to grow increasingly intense the more she drank. Will wrote down a description of the woman in his notes. He would need to find out who she was.

Will ordered the trout. It was perfectly pan-fried in butter, and absolutely delicious.

*

"Are you familiar with Newton's Third Law of Motion?" Professor Nedda Cake asked Detective Will Tenney.

"No, ma'am, I'm not," he answered.

The old woman's pale eyes gleamed in the sunlight streaming through her office window. Her velvety skin appeared translucent as a porcelain teacup.

"It tells us that for every action there is an equal and opposite reaction."

The old professor gazed at Will with a tranquil smile on her handsome face. If the eyes are windows on the soul, Will had the feeling he was gazing into great depths.

"Professor Cake, I understand there are members of your department who have reason to dislike Alan Sidebottom. Can you shed any light on that?"

Nedda Cake grinned.

"Detective, my best academic work is behind me. My powers of observation, however, do still seem to be in tact, and I am occasionally able to tease meaning out of facts," she said, pulling the cardigan sweater draped over her shoulders tighter. "Now, then."

"My husband, Frank, and I did some important work during our time at Oxford years ago. Alan Sidebottom was one of my husband's students. Frank always said Alan was one of his most gifted students. And possibly the laziest.   Ultimately, Alan co-opted some of our work for himself, and indeed, wrote a paper that helped land him a position at Cambridge. Frank never got over it. He died not long after that."

"So you see," she continued, dabbing at her nose with a handkerchief embroidered with a pale blue "N", "I have an awfully good motive for wanting to kill Alan. But of course I didn't. I believe in physics and mathematics, not in killing. I also believe that for every action there is an equal and opposite reaction, whether it applies to the physical world or the moral one. The universe takes care of it."

She peered at the young detective.

"Alan Sidebottom was an immoral man," Nedda continued. "I'm sorry he's dead, but then again, less wickedness in the world is quite a good thing for everyone." She leaned her head back against the chair and closed her eyes for a moment.

"Now then," she said. "I'm sure you must know by now that Alan also stole ideas from Mitchell Fender and published them under his own name. There's a motive.   Helen Mann was involved with Alan romantically many years ago. I think she may have been hoping to rekindle with him, but alas, he took no notice of her. A woman scorned always has a powerful motive for revenge, don't you find? And then there's dear Donald Gaylord, too clever for his own good. I overheard Alan saying something to Donald at tea one afternoon, which seemed to upset Donald deeply. Alan said something like, 'Tommy said to say hello'."

"What do think he meant?"

"No idea, dear boy. You'll have to work it out."

*

Will spent the rest of the day speaking to other members in the Physics & Astronomy Department.

Each had observed a different piece of the puzzle, and little by little, Will was beginning to see a picture emerge.

His next interview after Nedda Cake was with Lois Lieberman. Will knocked on her open door. Lois was talking on the phone, and motioned for Will to come in.

Will sat down and waited patiently, going over his notes. When Lois finished her call moments later, she apologized to Will, and offered any help she could to the investigation.

Will asked Lois about the cocktail party for Professor Sidebottom on the night of his arrival in New Guilford. Lois's first order of business was to cast aspersions on Sheila Dubin.

"You just don't wear a dress like that to a Department function," Lois sputtered, adjusting her pink tinted glasses.

"First of all, you don't wear a dress like that *anywhere* unless you're twenty-five years old. Which Sheila is, you know, exponentially *not*."

Will sat quietly, taking notes. Lois's office offered a stark contrast to Mitchell Fender's jumbled workspace, an observation he included in his notes. Her desk was tidy and uncluttered, and there was little in the way of decoration in the room. Black and white photographs of a beagle hung on the walls.

"That's Beechnut, my dog," Lois said, beaming. "She loves being photographed."

"Cute dog."

"You wouldn't think it, but she's a great watchdog. And she's an incredible athlete. She loves to swim and hike and stuff. Paolo and Francesca Rossetti, and Ravi Kapoor and I go hiking on the weekends sometimes. Beechnut always gets really excited."

"I imagine there's been a lot of conversation lately about the murder?" Will prodded.

"Yeah, we were having dinner the other night at Paolo and Francesca's house. Two names kept popping up: Mitchell Fender and Seth Dubin's wife, Sheila. We had all witnessed Mitchell's meltdown over the plagiarism thing with Alan Sidebottom last year. Then Mitch's wife left him, and things got pretty bad for Mitch. Anyway, we were thinking he has the best motive for killing Alan Sidebottom. But honestly, I don't think he has it in him to kill anybody. Not Mitch."

"Was Professor Fender's allegation of plagiarism legitimate?"

Lois Lieberman was silent for a moment. She ran her fingers through her short hair, fluffing it up.

"Mitchell definitely thought so. But it's hard to say. Mitchell only shared parts of his manuscript with us, and from the chapters I read I wouldn't be able to swear that Professor Sidebottom lifted from Mitchell's work. It's an open question," Lois said. "It's possible; I just can't say for sure. Mitch has his faults – like the rest of us – but when it comes right down to it, he's a decent guy."

"And Sheila Dubin?" Will said.

"The night of the party," Lois began, "a few of us noticed how strongly Sheila reacted when Alan Sidebottom was teasing Seth about his stammer. I'm telling you' her anger was epic. She practically turned colors, she was so mad. I mean, I would be mad, too, if Seth was my husband and somebody teased him about his stammer, but it's not that big a deal. Sidebottom was drinking, and nobody took anything he said that night very seriously. I just don't get why Sheila didn't throw it off. I would have."

"She happens to be a very pushy and ambitious woman," Lois continued. "She's dying for Seth to get on in the world. I think – a few of us thought – that she took the Sidebottom incident as a blow to Seth's career. Plus, I think she felt personally humiliated and even denigrated. Sheila is all about image. I wouldn't put anything past her if she felt somebody slighted her."

Chapter 13

Will stopped on his way into work at The Earl of Sandwich Café, a small New Guilford eatery popular with the town's old-timers. Will generally picked up something for lunch at Earl's, and once in a blue moon, stopped by for breakfast.

Hearty, homemade fare was cooked and served by Earl Dufresne, a retired tugboat captain. In a decidedly unfashionable neighborhood on the outskirts of New Guilford, Earl's clientele was more town than gown. So Will was surprised to see Edwina there. She was sitting at the counter in rapt concentration over a magazine article she had propped open against a napkin dispenser. A plate of blueberry pancakes sat half-eaten.

"Hello," Will said.

Edwina continued reading, her long eyelashes bumping against her bangs whenever she blinked.

"Excuse me?" he said, tapping lightly on her shoulder.

Edwina looked up, startled.

"Mind if I join you?" Will asked.

"Oh, it's you, hello. How goes the case?"

"We're making some progress. Slow—but steady. What are you reading, there?"

"Oh, it's physics stuff—you know—"

"Yeah? What's it about?" Will smiled.

"Uh, well, it's basically about parallel universes. There's this guy at M.I.T., Max Tegmark, amazing guy, very brilliant."

"Do you think I could understand the article if I read it?" Will said.

Edwina took a moment to think about this, although she knew the answer. She didn't wish to be rude, but facts were facts.

"Not really, no. But Professor Tegmark has a fabulous web site. You might enjoy that."

When Will's order of scrambled eggs with chili and cornbread came, Edwina peered curiously at the plate.

"That looks good," she said. "I'll have to try it next time."

"You're welcome to have a taste," Will said. "Here."

He held out a forkful of chili mixed with eggs. Edwina was uncertain whether he expected her to eat from the fork while he held it for her in mid-air, or whether she should hold up her own plate so he could tap the bite-full of food onto it. It all seemed somehow vaguely flirtatious, and Edwina was afraid of doing something clumsy. Finally she decided to take the fork from him and feed herself. This proved an awkward maneuver, and the food fell onto the floor.

"Good Lord," she said, feeling totally embarrassed. Her face infused with color, and she didn't know where to look. Will noticed that her freckles darkened when she blushed.

"No worries," Will said gallantly. "Here." He held his plate up for her to try another forkful of eggs and chili. Instead she picked up a spoon.

"Delicious!" she grinned.

After that, the conversation flowed easily. They traded stories on matters of local interest. Edwina expressed her opinion about the superiority of Dan's Bridge Market over the new supermarket in town.

"Who in their right mind wouldn't want to shop at a market where you can buy a six foot ladder along with your laundry detergent? Dan's has everything! And you know something else? That new super-ubermarket smells," Edwina said.

Will complained about the recent closing of one of two remaining independent bookshops in New Guilford, and Edwina commiserated. They shared stories about black bear sightings, and compared notes on where the best cross-country skiing was to be had nearby.

"Have you ever gone cross-country skiing at night?" Will said.

"At night? No, never have."

"I have this friend who lives up in Tunbridge. When he was in med school at Cushing, he used to have these 'midnight frenzy' parties in the wintertime. There had to be a full moon and a lot of snow, and then a bunch of us would get together and build a huge bonfire, and roast something—like a whole pig, or a road-kill deer. We'd go cross-country skiing in the moonlight, and then feast," Will said.

"Sounds like fun," Edwina said, suddenly looking at her watch.

"Damn! I'm nearly late for class!" she exclaimed, jumping off her stool.

Edwina grabbed her jacket and the magazine and dashed toward the door, turning to flash Will an indelible smile, before she disappeared into the lane.

*

Edwina drew back the curtains in her bedroom on Saturday morning and squinted at a sky of such brightness and clarity she could hardly wait to get her hands on it. The trembling leaves were resplendent with bold reds and oranges against the hydrangea blue sky. Edwina dressed hastily, packed a lunch, and sped on her bike toward the Boat House.

It was here on the river where she felt her own nature was in rhythm with nature itself. Here she could do nothing clumsy, or feel embarrassed or anxious. As she eased her kayak into the river, the waves reflected thousands of rapid pieces of sunlight, like some sort of light show, ongoing and ever changing.

Edwina headed downstream. She could smell wood smoke in the air from the nearby houses. Her thoughts soon melded with the motion of her paddle, the friction of the paddle meeting the water, the displacement of the water. Equations danced in her head, equations for fluid velocity and fluid density. Calculations ran through her mind about the force she was able to exert against the waves.

Some time later Edwina arrived at her private cove. She pulled the kayak onto the beach, and spread a wool blanket on the ground. Listening to the sounds of the leaves fluttering in the surrounding woods, she devoured a lunch of cheese and honey sandwiches, an apple, an orange, and a bottle of water. Afterwards she cleaned up the lunch remnants, rinsed her face and hands in the river water, and lay on the blanket with her damp face turned toward the sun. Edwina felt ineffably happy. Time seemed to distill into one, eternal moment. She had a sudden feeling of being connected to everything.

Her thoughts eventually turned to the Sidebottom business. Edwina reviewed the events of that last night when she had had dinner with Professor Sidebottom at the New World Tavern. How she had started to walk him back to campus. How he dashed off through the quiet streets of New Guilford, running like a man possessed. Edwina's guilt still needed assuaging.

I should have followed him on my bike. I could have caught up and found him. And then what? Fend off the killer? I could've been killed, too!

Edwina let this line of inquiry fall away.

I wonder why Charlotte Cadell looked at Sidebottom in such a hostile way at tea the afternoon before he died? He didn't seem to even notice her. Did she know him from before? She spoke in a strangely personal way about him that night at the New World . . . Poor Mitchel Fender! He certainly had a good reason for killing Sidebottom, but then again, everybody knew all about the plagiarism thing . . . what if somebody is trying to frame Mitchell? Professor Sidebottom was horrible to Seth Dubin, but Seth wouldn't hurt a fly . . . Sheila Dubin is another story, that woman gives me the willies . . . could some of the players be acting together in this thing? And what about Helen Mann, and her past with Professor Sidebottom?

Edwina rolled onto her stomach, resting her head on folded arms. A continuous breeze softly ruffled her hair. Her dark fleece jacket had absorbed so much heat from the sun it felt like a hot water bottle, and she soon fell asleep. When she awoke a short while later, a doe and two fawns stood at the edge of the woods staring at Edwina, waiting for her to make a move so they would know if this human animal was friend or foe.

Chapter 14

Will set off for Boston at noon on Monday, supplied with a thermos of coffee, a large bottle of water, and two turkey, stuffing, and cranberry sandwiches from Earl's Café. His first stop would be to interview Donald Gaylord's wife. Will had called the day before and left a message for her to meet him at the Gaylord home at two o'clock. He had not heard back from her, and hoped she would be there.

He turned on the radio, but quickly turned it off again. He wanted to concentrate on the case.

There was no shortage of motives. Mitchell Fender and Donald Gaylord hovered near the top of Will's list. Alan Sidebottom's alleged theft of Mitchell's original research had surely damaged, if not ruined, Mitchell's chances of tenure and promotion, and cost him a raise in salary. Maybe even cost him his marriage. Perhaps the most enduring loss to Mitchell Fender was the respect of his colleagues.

And Donald Gaylord? He got Detective Tenney's hackles up. Surely that was a barometer for something. Donald Gaylord was too ambitious, too slick for his own good, and he had behaved in a guilty manner from the get-go, or at least, a nervous one. Then there was the unfinished business of the 'Tommy' reference that had visibly upset Donald when Nedda Cake overheard Professor Sidebottom mention it to Donald that day in the library.

And there was Nedda Cake, herself. One scenario was that Professor Cake had decided her last meaningful contribution to society would be to avenge the wrongs Alan Sidebottom had done to her late husband, and to all the other people he had ever hurt. Maybe she calculated the probability of getting away with his death was in her favor. Would anybody really believe that an angelic-looking old lady, who happened to be a prominent theoretical physicist would murder a colleague?

Then there was another possibility, this one involving Helen Mann. Jealous of Alan Sidebottom's celebrity status—angered by being snubbed by him at the party—her romantic aspirations toward Alan Sidebottom dashed . . . too many blows to Helen Mann's estimable ego? People had killed for less.

And what of Sheila Dubin? Lois Lieberman had voiced her suspicions of Seth Dubin's wife loud and clear. And several other people present at the party had sensed Sheila Dubin's fury toward Professor Sidebottom. So far all of Will's visits and phone calls to Sheila Dubin had gone unanswered, unreturned.

And what of the priggish librarian, Charlotte Cadell, who seemed like an implosion waiting to happen? Perhaps it already had, with Alan Sidebottom as its target. Motive?

Will arrived at the Gaylord's home just before two o'clock. 6509 High Drive was a charming and well-kept little two-story, stone and wood house, in a quiet Boston suburb. Mature sycamore trees tinkled with chimes. A flagstone walkway led to the front door, where a pair of black urns was planted with coleus, ivy and chrysanthemums.

Will parked his car at the curb. Sidewalks ran along both sides of the quiet, tree-lined street. The sweet smell of the sycamores wafted through the air.

A man in his thirties with an athletic build answered the door. He wore a flour-dusted apron over jeans and a gray tee shirt.

"Is this the home of Donald Gaylord?"

"Yes, it is," the man answered. "Can I help you?"

"I have an appointment to meet Mrs. Gaylord," Will said, showing identification. "I left a message yesterday."

"You're looking at her," the man laughed. "Come on in."

"I apologize for the mistake. I didn't realize, sorry," said a flustered Will.

"No worries. None of Don's friends at the college know about me. Don prefers it that way," the man replied easily, shaking hands with Will. "Jimmy Lopez. Please, take a seat."

The décor was formal but welcoming. A sofa and pair of club chairs were covered in chintz fabric bearing a classical motif of urns and swags. Drapes made of the same material were pulled back and held in place by cherry wood rosettes at tall windows on either side of a marble fireplace. An elegant mantle displayed a collection of English pottery. The house smelled of baking.

"Don told me about the death at school. I assume that's why you're here, detective?"

"Yes, it is. I wondered if you had ever met Alan Sidebottom? It seems Professor Gaylord knew him years ago, when he was a student of Professor Sidebottom's in England."

"No, I never met him. Don has mentioned him once or twice, but that's about it," Jimmy said. "By the way, can I offer you a cup of coffee or something? Jimmy's manner was relaxed and genial.

"No thanks," Will replied.

"May I ask you why Professor Gaylord keeps your relationship and living arrangement a secret?"

Jimmy laughed.

"Don's kind of an old-fashioned guy. He's afraid it might hurt his career. He's got his eye on running the department up at Cushing some day, and he's worried being outed would ruin his chances," Jimmy said.

"We have a nice, discreet circle of friends here in Boston," Jimmy continued. "Don is here just about every weekend. It works out pretty well."

"We used to argue about it in the beginning. Now I tease him about it. I tell him when he gets to be Head of the Department I'll throw a big, fabulous party in New Guilford and invite all our friends up from Boston," Jimmy said.

"How long have the two of you been together?"

"We played football together in college. We've been together ever since."

"Do you ever visit Professor Gaylord in New Guilford?"

The question had hit a nerve. Jimmy's easy-going manner faltered for a moment.

"Couple of times," Jimmy said. "When Don first got hired there, I went up on the weekends, but he just wasn't comfortable with it."

Jimmy smiled broadly. "C'est la guerre," he shrugged.

They continued chatting while Jimmy showed Will around the house and the garden. They ended up in the kitchen, where the aromatic, yeasty smell of fresh bread swirled through the air. Jimmy filled a brown lunch bag of warm scones and insisted Will take them, which he was only too happy to do.

Will's mind started to race when he got back to the car. There was a new wrinkle in the case. What if Jimmy Lopez weren't as easy-going as he presented?

It's possible that Jimmy suspected Donald Gaylord of having an intimate relationship with the famous Professor Sidebottom. How could Jimmy *not* feel jealous, with Donald up at college all week? Jimmy understood how ambitious Donald was. Could Donald possibly have decided to advance his career by cozying up to Sidebottom? What if the amiable Jimmy Lopez had traveled unnoticed to New Guilford and killed Alan Sidebottom in a jealous fit? No one would recognize Jimmy Lopez. No one would take special notice of him—he could have moved around the Cushing campus easily, without causing suspicion. It occurred to Will that Donald Gaylord might even suspect Jimmy, and that's why Donald had been behaving so nervously.

Will wolfed down two scones as he drove to the next destination, and parked his car on a busy street in the heart of Cambridge.

The window in front of Salon Jean-Paul was draped with festoons of ivory-colored chiffon so passersby could not peer inside. Will entered the salon and felt immediately out of his element from the cacophony and clamor, the loud music and bright, glaring lights. Because it wasn't practical for salons to have carpeting or curtains or upholstered seats because of easy staining from the chemical products, there was nothing to absorb the sound. A din and clatter of hair dryers, blaring music and loud conversation ricocheted off the hard surfaces inside the salon. Will could hardly wait to leave the punishing atmosphere of sensory overload.

Helen Mann's stylist was a pleasant young woman named Anne Marie Prestopino. Will explained his reason for being there and showed Anne Marie his police identification. She invited him into the back room where they could speak more privately. Anne Marie pushed aside a curtain hanging in the doorway, and Will followed her. Floor to ceiling metal shelving held products and supplies. There was a small refrigerator in one corner, and a table next to it with a double coffee maker, and a hot water dispenser for tea. The seating was a scattering of low wooden stools. Will perched tentatively on one.

"How long have you been cutting Helen Mann's hair?"

"Cutting and coloring, actually. Let me see. I've been here for five years, and Helen was one of my first clients, so I'd say, maybe four and a half or five years. She's a nice lady."

Anne Marie, wore a crisp, black smock over jeans, and sat comfortably with her legs extended straight in front of her and crossed at the ankles.

"Does Dr. Mann ever discuss her private life?"

Anne Marie thought for a moment.

"A little bit, yeah. You'd be amazed by the things people talk about sometimes when they're in the chair or at the sink—really personal stuff—affairs, divorce, abortions, even. It wasn't anything like that with Helen, though. You know, nothing all that personal. But I get the feeling that she's kind of lonely," she said.

"Anything in particular you can recall her talking about? Any names?" Will asked, taking notes.

"Mostly she talks about work. About the pressure and the demands of her job – how hard it is dealing with so many big egos, stuff like that. But the last time she was here she was talking about getting back together with an old flame. She seemed excited about it, too. She was talking about not letting the important things slip through her fingers. And I knew exactly what she meant, because I was dating this guy for two years—Max—and I wish I'd never broken up with him. My mother didn't like him because he wasn't Catholic, and I let her talk me into breaking up. Nicest guy I ever met. I can't believe I did that."

They chatted for a few more minutes. Anne Marie offered Will a trim on the house, and he politely declined.

"Have you ever considered highlights?" she said. "You would look fantastic with some blond highlights. You know, not too much, just a little pop of color at the front."

Will wasn't sure if she was kidding or not.

"I'm probably not really a highlight kind of guy," he said smiling, "but I'll think about it. Thanks."

Chapter 15

Edwina awoke early, and looked out the window. The mornings were getting colder, this one gray and overcast. Dressing with warm layers, she recalled countless frosty childhood bike rides, bundled up against the bracing chill, armed against the cold with the delirious feeling of freedom.

The trees were mostly bare now, and the nearly empty streets were covered in crunching leaves. Edwina pedaled casually, soothed by the peace and quiet and fresh air. She stopped at Dan's Bridge Market to pick up a few groceries and sundry items, and stowed the provisions safely in the locking saddlebags on her bike.

Edwina rode home via Cushing, along the path that rambled through the hundreds of acres belonging to the college. Each time she rode on campus she noticed something new or different in the landscape.

She squinted her eyes to focus on two familiar figures some distance away. Nedda Cake and Mitchell Fender were strolling together near the Medical School Clinic. Edwina wondered if she should stop to say 'hello', but thought better of it. She didn't wish to intrude on a private moment, if that was what they were having.

Edwina circled around and headed back toward the clinic, curiosity getting the better of her. Nedda and Mitchell were nowhere in sight. Edwina locked her bike and walked into the clinic.

She approached the Information desk.

"Hello," Edwina said. "I was supposed to meet my uncle and my grandmother here after their appointment. Do you know if they've come out, yet?"

"What was the name?" asked the woman at Information.

"Mitchell Fender and Nedda Cake."

The woman checked her computer.

"Mr. Fender's appointment with Dr. Swisher was for ten o'clock. Let me check and see if they're still in with the doctor."

"Thank-you very much," Edwina said.

"I'm sorry," the woman said, returning a few moments later, "I'm afraid they left the clinic a short while ago."

"Oh, well, I'm sure I can catch up with them. Thanks," said Edwina.

She jumped on her bike and rode home. Edwina dashed inside the house, leaving all the shopping items in the saddlebags on her bike. She immediately sat down at the computer, and went to the Cushing Medical School Clinic web site. She typed in the name of Dr. Swisher.

A Dr. Elizabeth Swisher came up. Neurosurgeon.

Edwina sat back in the chair.

Neurosurgeon, she thought. *Poor Mitchell. I wonder what's going on? I hope he's okay. What was Nedda doing with him? Moral support?*

She considered contacting Nedda to ask, but how would Edwina explain how she knew about Mitchell's appointment with Dr. Swisher in the first place?

She would just have to leave this piece of information alone for the time being.

*

Edwina hatched a plan. Based on her speculation that Charlotte Cadell knew more about Department goings-on than anybody else, possibly even including information about Alan Sidebottom's murder, Edwina considered Charlotte an untapped resource.

Charlotte presented as genteel and correct—the dignified spinster librarian—but Edwina knew that still waters ran deep, and that there was more to Charlotte than she let people know about, probably even herself. The idea was to gain Charlotte's confidence somehow.

Edwina's plan was to linger inconspicuously in the library until an opportunity presented itself to engage Charlotte in conversation. Edwina would do her best to ingratiate herself, and hope that things progressed from there.

When she had finished teaching her morning class, Edwina stopped by her office to gather a few things and headed downstairs to the Sanborn House Library. She was ready to launch Operation Charlotte.

Edwina set with her laptop at the far end one of the long, study tables. From her vantage point she could survey the whole library. To give the scene added verisimilitude Edwina wandered toward the stacks and made of show of searching out specific titles, finally returning to the table with books in tow.

Charlotte kept busy. When she wasn't working at her desk on the computer or on the phone, she was re-shelving books or helping a student locate information. After nearly an hour of this, Edwina began to feel foolish, began to doubt her plan.

But not quite ready to give up, Edwina returned the not-very-interesting books she had taken off the shelves, and wandered up the spiral staircase where she could peruse the balcony library collection. Something in the biography section caught her eye, and Edwina was soon engrossed in a book about the nineteenth century Swedish physicist, Anders Jonas Angstrom. She sat on the carpeted floor in the canyon of stacks, absorbed in the story of the man who founded spectroscopy, and who was the first person to ever examine the spectrum of the aurora borealis.

"Excuse me, Edwina?" someone whispered.

"Edwina?" they repeated.

Edwina looked up.

"I'm sorry if I startled you," Charlotte said. "I was wondering if I could ask a favor of you? It's just that I won't be able to be here tomorrow afternoon—there's a librarians conference I can't get out of—I hate asking you this, but could you possibly set up afternoon tea tomorrow? I know it's a terrible imposition, but I wasn't sure who else to ask. It's a pretty simple procedure, and I could show you where everything is—"

"I'd be happy to, Charlotte," Edwina answered quickly. "It's no trouble at all."

"Would now be a convenient time for me to show you where everything is? I was just on my way downstairs to the kitchen."

Edwina could hardly believe the serendipity of the situation. She eagerly followed Charlotte downstairs to the basement, flush with a feeling of adventure. In all her years at Cushing, Edwina had never been into the basement of Sanborn House. All sorts of images flew through her mind—rotting laboratory tables cluttered with antiquated and arcane scientific instruments, covered in layers of dust and cobwebs, and rusted out . . .

In fact there was nothing very interesting at all, just a dreary kitchen with no windows. The lighting consisted of two fluorescent tubes running along a low ceiling. It was a depressing room, dingy and airless. Everything was brown—the floor, the cabinets and walls. The only bright color was an orange metal kettle sitting atop an ancient looking stove.

"What an absolute dungeon!" Edwina said.

"Oh, it's not too bad," Charlotte said. "I'm in and out of here pretty quickly."

"I'll tell you what I think," Edwina blurted in a flash of inspiration, "I think we should buy some paint and get this place spruced up. We could do it on the weekend. It's not very big—we could probably knock it off in a day."

Charlotte grew animated. "What a lovely idea," she said, gazing around the miserable little kitchen, at the stained ceiling, and peeling cabinets.

"I hope you won't regret your offer!" Charlotte said.

Charlotte walked Edwina through the preparations for tea, which were largely self-explanatory. She showed her where everything was kept—the cups and saucers, spoons, tea bags, sugar bowl, baked goods and trays. The ornate brass samovar for the hot water was sitting in a corner.

"It's an awful lot of stuff to lug upstairs, isn't it?" Edwina said.

Charlotte smiled and pointed to the wall.

"No lugging required," she said. And with that, she reached out and took hold of a barely visible panel in the wall, with a small, black handle. She pulled upwards on the panel to reveal a dumb waiter.

*

Using the ample space inside her backpack, the roomy saddlebags on her bike, plus the basket on the handlebars, Edwina was able to transport all the painting supplies to Sanborn House. She got to the library just after ten o'clock Saturday morning.

Charlotte had not yet arrived, but Edwina wanted to get started. She set about covering the floor with plastic sheeting. Next she wiped down the walls and cabinets with a sponge and spray cleaner. Overly pleased with herself for remembering to bring a flathead screwdriver to open the paint cans Edwina stirred and poured the paint into shallow rolling pans. She had chosen a lively, orange sherbet color in high gloss finish.

When Charlotte had still not shown up half an hour later, Edwina began to grow concerned. Edwina checked her phone for messages and to see if somehow, by chance, she had Charlotte's number. She didn't.

Edwina went upstairs to look for Charlotte's number on her desk in the library. She hated to snoop through Charlotte's things, but it seemed important. Finally Edwina found Charlotte's contact information and dialed her number. Charlotte did not answer her phone, and Edwina started to feel anxious. Charlotte, after all, was nothing if not punctual.

With the mystery of Alan Sidebottom's death still casting a shadow on Sanborn House, Edwina ran downstairs on a feverish whim. She threw open the dumb-waiter, half expecting to find Charlotte's crumpled body stuffed inside. Happily, it wasn't.

Just then Edwina heard someone coming down the basement steps.

"I am so sorry I'm late!" Charlotte panted. "I had a flat tire and I had to wait for the auto club to come and change it for me. I really am so sorry—I feel just awful!"

Edwina was relieved and amused to see Charlotte dressed in old khaki pants, an oversized flannel shirt, and Converse sneakers. So different from her usual garb of sweaters and tweed skirts. Her hair was even fixed in pigtails.

"What do you think of the color?" Edwina asked, indicating the partially painted wall.

Charlotte gazed at the swath of glossy orange sherbet color.

"Oh my goodness! It's wonderful, so bright and cheerful! It's perfect!"

"This color is going to make the most incredible difference," Charlotte beamed, picking up a paint roller.

"Honestly, it's going to make coming down here so much more pleasant! Especially now, with all the Alan Sidebottom business, the whole place seems gloomier than ever," Charlotte said.

Edwina's ears twitched. She was bursting to approach the topic of the murder, but did not want to seem over anxious about it.

"I'm glad you approve of the color. It was between this, and bubblegum pink," Edwina said. "And another thing I was thinking, is that we could change out the lighting. We could get a perfectly nice, cheap lighting fixture for the ceiling, and get rid of these horrible fluorescent tubes."

"What a good idea!" Charlotte said, swabbing paint onto a wall.

Edwina allowed a few minutes to pass.

"Speaking of Professor Sidebottom," she ventured, "What do you make of it all? Poor man, coming all the way to Cushing, just to get murdered."

Charlotte was quiet for a moment. Edwina wondered if she had overstepped.

"It's horrible," Charlotte said. "Everyone looks at each other a little differently now, as if everybody suspects everybody else. It's poisoned the atmosphere around here."

"Oh, I agree," Edwina said. "There's definitely suspicion in the air. I mean, to think that we could actually have a killer in our midst . . . "

"It's getting fume-y in here," Charlotte said. "I'm going to run upstairs and get the electric fan from my desk. Be right back."

Trying not to force the conversation, Edwina let the proceedings relax into a companionable silence, with the two women occasionally remarking on their progress, or how good the new color looked, or how much more cheerful the basement would be.

They finished by early afternoon.

"I'm famished," Charlotte said. "I'd love to take you to lunch to repay you for your hard work. And speaking of repayment, I'll get the department to reimburse you for the paint and everything. I can't tell you how much I appreciate this, Edwina."

"Don't bother! I charged all this stuff to the college. But lunch sounds great—I'm starved," Edwina replied.

They rinsed out the brushes, rollers and pans, folded the plastic sheeting, and along with the extra paint, put everything in a small storage area just off the kitchen. The women stood in the doorway, admiring their work. The dull little room looked almost inviting with its shiny new orange sherbet walls and cupboards.

"Let's leave the fan going down here. It'll help dry the paint faster," Edwina suggested.

They decided on the New World for lunch, and ordered wine while they waited for their food to arrive. Drinking wine in the middle of the day and dressed in paint-spattered work clothes, Charlotte seemed more interesting than the guarded persona she exhibited at work. Edwina regarded Charlotte in this new incarnation, and wondered what other layers and colors Charlotte might reveal. She wondered, too, if this transformation in Charlotte was the result of the change of venue—being away from the professional restraints of Sanborn House—or the wine, or both, or something else altogether.

Fine lines of sadness and despair had etched themselves around Charlotte's delicate eyes on along her cheeks. But she slowly became more animated the more she drank and the more she talked, until these fine lines began to read more like determination than resignation.

"I feel sorry for some of these Cushing kids," Charlotte said. "They are so used to having all the advantages in life, but soon enough they'll find out how hard life really is, and how much is just luck. They take for granted that they will achieve all their goals, but most of them won't be able to deal with it when things don't go their way."

Edwina kept quiet. She wondered if Charlotte was speaking autobiographically, as people so often do, without even realizing it.

"I, myself, was a promising physics student years ago, ready to set the world on fire. Did you know that, Edwina? No, I didn't think so. Then I met a young man, also a student in the department, and we fell in love. We imagined a life together in academia, with children, and a house, and a picket fence. We got engaged."

Charlotte ordered another glass of wine.

"One fine spring morning he broke off our engagement. He wouldn't even say why. He gave me this." Charlotte held her hand out for Edwina to see the Victorian ring Will Tenney had admired.

"You can imagine how I felt," Charlotte went on. "I dropped out of school. I began to suffer from depression, and had to move in with my parents because I couldn't—or wouldn't—look after myself. I never finished my degree."

"I'm awfully sorry, Charlotte," Edwina said.

"The reason I'm telling you this," Charlotte said, "is that eventually I did find out why he broke off our engagement. You see, my fiancé was a student of Alan Sidebottom at the time. We both were," Charlotte grimaced.

Aha! Edwina thought. *I knew she must have known Professor Sidebottom somehow!*

Charlotte seemed to be waiting for Edwina to say something.

"What an incredible coincidence," Edwina ventured.

"I don't think you quite understand," Charlotte said. "The reason my fiancé broke off our engagement was *because* of Alan Sidebottom. Alan worked both sides of the street, if you see what I mean. He seduced my boyfriend. He broke us up by persuading my boyfriend that he was gay."

Edwina could not think what to say.

"So you see," Charlotte continued, "I have a terrific motive for killing Alan Sidebottom. He did ruin my life, after all. But, of course, I didn't. I would have liked to, but I don't have the courage."

"Have you told the police all this?" Edwina said.

"No. What if they didn't believe me? What if they think I killed Alan Sidebottom?"

"But it's bound to come out in the course of their investigation," Edwina said. "I think it would be a lot better if this information came from you."

Edwina suddenly felt light-headed from the wine. The improbable idea suddenly struck her that underneath the prim façade of Charlotte Cadell there might lurk a raving lunatic. What if Charlotte did kill Alan Sidebottom, and now she would have to kill Edwina to prevent her from telling the police?

Get a grip! Edwina thought. *Be rational! The librarian at Sanborn House is hardly likely to be a homicidal lunatic!*

"Listen, Charlotte," Edwina said as calmly as she could manage, "I would be happy to go with you to the police station so you can explain all of this. I think you'd feel much better."

I know I would, Edwina thought.

"Maybe you're right," Charlotte said, draining her third glass of Pinot Grigio. "'The truth will out', I suppose."

Chapter 16

Edwina stopped at the police station Monday morning. The annoying woman at the front desk showed no flicker of recognition.

"Is Detective Tenney in?" Edwina said.

"In regards to what?"

"It's about the professor's death—up at the college," Edwina said.

The receptionist picked up the phone and called Will's extension.

"Name?" she asked.

"Edwina Goodman."

"Edwina Goodman wishes to see you," she spoke into the phone. "Again."

Edwina now knew the way, and Will was waiting in the hall for her.

"Nice to see you. Come in," he said.

Edwina took more notice of Will's office this time. She had been in too much of a frazzle the last time. Photographs of mountainous landscapes taken in different seasons decorated the white walls. Stacks of *Professional Investigator Magazines* and law enforcement journals crowded the bookshelves, alongside box files. A faded jean jacket hung on the back of the door.

Edwina sat down in front of his desk.

"Listen, I know I'm supposed to be minding my own beeswax and not poking my nose into the Sidebottom murder," she started.

"Uh-huh."

"But I do have some information which I think might be useful," Edwina said.

"Okay. I'm listening."

Edwina pushed her bangs to one side. She briefly wondered if Will would be mad at her for not backing off playing amateur detective, the way he had asked her to. Will stood facing her, leaning against the front of the desk, his hands in his trouser pockets.

"I had lunch with Charlotte Cadell, the librarian at Sanborn House," she began. "I never knew any of this before, but it turns out she was engaged to be married years ago, when she was in college. Studying physics. She and her boyfriend were students of Professor Sidebottom. Apparently Professor Sidebottom made a play for Charlotte's fiancé, who then broke off his engagement to Charlotte. Charlotte never married, and she blames Sidebottom for ruining her life."

Will peered at Edwina.

"You know that ring she wears? The fiancé gave it to her. She told me she never takes it off. I told Charlotte—I tried to be very insistent—that she should come in here and tell you all this, but she was afraid she would become suspect number one. Don't you think that's an awfully good motive?" Edwina said.

Will felt simultaneously irritated and impressed. Irritated that Edwina had not taken his caution to heart about the dangers of poking around the investigation. But impressed by her results. She was a force of nature, he figured, and it would take a lot more than his admonitions to change the course of her actions.

"Possibly, yeah," he answered. "And when I spoke with Louis Canevari at The New World, he described witnessing an argument between Charlotte Cadell and Donald Gaylord on the night you were all at the restaurant, the day Alan Sidebottom was discovered dead. So I have to wonder if Donald Gaylord and Charlotte knew each others' secrets, and if they were threatening to tell the police what they knew."

"What do you mean about Charlotte Cadell knowing Donald Gaylord's "secret?" Edwina asked.

Will hesitated. He found Edwina's ease in thinking outside the box invaluable. Nonetheless, she was not officially part of the investigation, and he knew that sharing information with her would be bending the rules. There was also the problem of divulging confidential information about one of her colleagues. Edwina had unwittingly rendered Will uncharacteristically ambivalent about right and wrong. But his sense of trust in her overwhelmed these considerations, and he took the plunge.

"This is strictly confidential, okay?" he said at last. "It doesn't go any further than this office, right?"

"Of course!" Edwina said.

"Right. I was curious about Professor Gaylord's long-distance marriage arrangement," Will said, "so I drove to Boston to speak with his wife. The Gaylords live in a pretty house on a quiet street in one of the nicest suburbs in Boston."

"Come to find out," Will continued, "Donald Gaylord's better half is a guy named Jimmy Lopez. They played football together at Yale. Been together ever since."

A wide-eyed Edwina was speechless.

"So I have to wonder if an ambitious guy like Donald Gaylord would kill to keep his secret safe? Jimmy Lopez confirmed for me that Professor Gaylord worries about the truth of his personal life getting out because he's convinced it would damage his career. I'm thinking Alan Sidebottom knew all about Donald Gaylord from Donald's student days in England, and was planning to expose him. Maybe just for spite. Or for the fun of it, who knows? Professor Gaylord was probably hoping that Sidebottom's memory was pickled, and that he had forgotten all about him. But then when Gaylord realized Sidebottom remembered him, he had to kill him. Professor Cake said something when I interviewed her that supports this idea. She said one afternoon in the library she heard Sidebottom say something to Donald Gaylord like, 'Tommy says hello', and Donald went nuts."

"That must be the reason Donald carries on with Sheila Dubin," Edwina said slowly. "It's just a cover. But that doesn't take Sheila out of the running. She had her own reason for hating Professor Sidebottom. Maybe she and Donald Gaylord did it together."

"She's not at the top of my list, but I guess it's possible. Then again, I'm not counting out Helen Mann," Will said. "'Hell hath no fury like a woman scorned', and I have good reason to believe Helen was hoping to rekindle her old romance with Sidebottom. When Professor Sidebottom blew her off at the party that night, Helen became enraged. Not only did Sidebottom fail to acknowledge his 'special past' with Helen Mann, I don't think he even acknowledged her. He may not have recognized her. Now that's got to be quite a blow to the ego. Especially if you're Helen Mann."

Edwina regarded Will intently, trying to keep pace with his astonishing narrative.

"Then we've got Mitchell Fender," Will went on. "His reasons for hating Sidebottom are epic—the guy stole Mitchell Fender's career out from under him. And that may have caused Mitchell's wife to leave him. The problem is, a neighbor confirmed that Dr. Fender was home all night on Monday, as he claimed to be."

"But wait a minute," Edwina said, "If Professor Sidebottom was poisoned by digitalis, then it's possible someone could have given it to him at any time—in a box of chocolates, or in a bottle of wine—isn't that right? The killer wouldn't care *when* Alan ate the chocolates or drank the wine—just so long as he did!"

"You're absolutely right," Will said. "Except that we didn't find anything like a box of chocolates, empty or otherwise, or an empty wine or liquor bottle. No evidence of anything suspicious ingested, whatsoever. Besides which, there was practically nothing in his stomach. You told me, yourself, that he didn't eat any dinner that night at the restaurant. There was a bottle of scotch at the cottage, but it hadn't been opened. And nothing in the fridge had been tampered with."

"What about at the restaurant?" Edwina said. "The whole department knew Professor Sidebottom and I were going to The New World that night for dinner. Couldn't someone have slipped the digitalis into his drink?" she said.

"I interviewed all the patrons who were there that night, and the staff," Will replied. "Nobody was aware of Professor Sidebottom or knew who he was."

"But couldn't someone have slipped in the back way, bribed a waiter or a busboy to put the digitalis into Alan's drink, and then duck out?" Edwina persisted.

"It's possible, but it's a stretch."

Edwina and Will sat looking at each other in the quiet office. The muffled sounds of traffic filtered in through the closed windows.

"Mild-mannered Seth Dubin has got motive, too," Will said. "Think about it. The guy finally meets his hero, after years of reading his books and working his way up in the same field. Then Sidebottom humiliates him in public, right in front of his wife, his students, and his colleagues."

"No way, Seth wouldn't harm anybody!" Edwina said. "He's one of the nicest guys around. It's impossible."

"I saw him having lunch with a woman the other day at The New World," Will said. "He looked none too happy. What does his wife look like?"

Edwina described Sheila Dubin.

"Yeah, that was her," he said.

"Now there's a thought," Edwina said. "Everybody says she wears the pants in that house. What if Sheila somehow forced Seth into her crazy plan for revenge? Somehow forced him to be her accomplice? And also, what about my idea that Sheila could be the daughter of Helen Mann and Alan Sidebottom?"

"I looked into that," Will said. "It was a no-go."

"Too bad," Edwina said, "such a nice theory."

The two sat quietly, thinking. Will gazed out the window at the view of backs of buildings, and delivery docks and alleyways crowded with trucks and dumpsters.

"Tell me about Professor Cake," he said.

"I know what you're thinking," Edwina replied. "That she has history with Alan Sidebottom. That Professor Sidebottom plagiarized from Frank Cake years ago in England. But why in the world would she want to exact revenge after all this time, for something that happened all those years ago? She's coming to the end of a brilliant career. Her husband has been gone a long time. She's retiring next year when she turns ninety. Why would she ruin all that?"

"Opportunity, maybe?" replied Will. "If it's true that Sidebottom plagiarized Professor Cake's late husband and drove him to an early grave, maybe she's dreamed of revenge for a long time. Maybe Sidebottom showing up at Cushing was a golden opportunity for Nedda Cake. Who knows? Maybe she even considered the arrival of Sidebottom a gift from her late husband, an opportunity to settle the score."

"Well, it might look good on paper," Edwina said. "I can see that. But the thing is, taking somebody's life goes against everything Nedda Cake believes in. She's a dyed-in-the-wool pacifist. She doesn't even eat meat, for goodness sake! It's simply not in her nature," Edwina said.

"But her age could figure in as a factor the other way, couldn't it?" Will said. "How much have you got to lose when you're ninety, with a full and successful life behind you? Maybe she sees herself as her husband's avenger? Maybe she saw taking out Sidebottom as her ultimate purpose in life—her swan song?"

Edwina was quiet.

"It's possible," she said at last. "But it's doubtful. She's not like that. She doesn't harbor grudges or live in the past. She's a real, old-fashioned existentialist— she lives each day as if it was the *only day*, and she makes her choices accordingly. She would never want to finish her life as a murderer. No way."

"What about as a hero?" asked Will.

He thought Edwina was being sentimental, that her view of Nedda Cake lacked objectivity. He decided it would be more practical to leave this avenue of speculation alone. There was no arguing with sentiment.

"Well, at this moment," Will said, "I'm looking hard at Donald Gaylord. Whether information about his private life would have hurt his career or not, I have no idea – but he definitely thought he had a lot to lose if word got out. I'm thinking Donald saw Professor Sidebottom sometime between when you and Professor Sidebottom parted company after dinner on his last night alive, and the time he was found dead at the cottage the following morning.   Donald could have administered the fatal dose of digitalis easily enough in a drink.   He could have left Sheila Dubin at the Inn, after their cozy dinner, and gone over to campus for a nightcap with Alan Sidebottom at the cottage."

Edwina wanted to tell Will about seeing Mitchell Fender and Nedda Cake at the clinic on Saturday, but she hesitated.   She didn't want to implicate Mitchell or Nedda, but the fact of Mitchell's health problems was possibly relevant.   Edwina did not want to seem like more of a busybody than she already did.   But data is data, and it's no good ignoring it.

"There's one other thing," she said.

"Uh-huh?"

"I happened to be riding my bike on Saturday, and I saw Mitchell Fender and Nedda Cake at the College Clinic together."

"Uh-huh?"

"Mitchell had an appointment with a neurosurgeon, and although I don't know what his condition is, I was thinking that if it's something serious—and I hope it isn't—but if it *is* something serious, his illness might have an effect on his willingness to do something rash. Like killing Professor Sidebottom.   If Mitchell is dying—and I hope to goodness he isn't—maybe he felt he had nothing to lose, and so he decided to take revenge on Sidebottom for stealing his work."

Will regarded Edwina with curiosity.

"Did you speak with Dr. Fender and Dr. Cake at the clinic?" he asked.

"No, they had gone before I had a chance," Edwina replied.

"Then, how do you know his appointment was with a neurosurgeon?"

"Right.   That's a good question."

Too late to turn back now.

"Well, I thought it might be important to the investigation, so I went into the clinic and said I was his niece, and that I was supposed to meet him there, and asked if he was still in with the doctor. When the lady at Information checked, she told me Mitchell had already left his appointment with Dr. Swisher. So when I got home I looked up Dr. Swisher and found out she's a neurosurgeon." Edwina said.

When Will was finished feeling annoyed by Edwina's persistent snooping, he couldn't help smiling.

"Well done," he said.

Chapter 17

Edwina's mind was racing when she left the station. All she wanted to do was think—if only she could take the whole day off just to think! It felt to her as if the facts surrounding the case were poised to fall into place, to distill themselves into greater clarity. The prospect of teaching a class in introductory physics to a group of barely interested, non-science majors made her groan.

As soon as class let out Edwina cycled to the Boat House. There was a lot to think about, and it was no good thinking about it in dribs and drabs. Connections needed to be made. She needed an uninterrupted chunk of time to work them out, and paddling would be just the thing. She was greedy for solitude.

She launched the kayak into the frosty water. Despite the air being much nippier at river level, Edwina felt herself beginning to relax, felt the brain cylinders getting fired up. She zipped up her fleece jacket, fished a wool hat out of one pocket and a pair of gloves from the other. She took hold of the paddle and started downriver.

Focusing on the river seemed to tame her jumbled thoughts. The sunlight played leapfrog across the tops of the small waves, and the white noise of rushing water sounded a soothing balm. Edwina gazed across miles of trees blazing with color, and breathed in whiffs of wood smoke in the cold, afternoon air.

She began to consider the murder of Alan Sidebottom. She reflected on her conversations with

Will, with Nedda Cake, and with Charlotte Cadell. She thought about the mighty list of suspects. Donald Gaylord, Mitchell Fender, Helen Mann, Charlotte, Seth and Sheila Dubin, Jimmy Lopez—even her beloved Nedda Cake. According to Will, they all had motive and opportunity. Was there anyone they were leaving out?

As she turned over scenario after scenario in her mind, pursuing all sorts of ideas, down a multitude of bunny trails, the facts of the case as she knew them would not add up. She could not get the math to work. If all the pieces of the equation did not fit perfectly, you had to keep digging.

When dark clouds began to roll in from the west, Edwina became conscious of the afternoon growing colder. After a while she decided she had better call it a day. Finding a good spot to back paddle, Edwina turned the kayak around and headed back upriver toward the Boat House.

Back at her office in Sanborn House Edwina picked up a piece of chalk from the desk and approached the chalkboard. She spun the board on its axis to the reverse side.

In order to connect the dots you have to collect the dots, she recalled one of her professors saying. She wrote on the board:

> 1. Alan Sidebottom. Fatal heart attack brought on by digitalis overdose + drunk. Alcoholic – academic celebrity – wealthy – philanderer (men + women) – various ex-wives and children (estranged)–has possibly or probably plagiarized from at least Mitchell Fender and Frank Cake. Affair with Helen years ago. Affair with Charlotte's fiancé. Last movements – Monday afternoon tea (anyone could have

slipped a fatal dose of digitalis in his tea);
dinner at New   World with me (the whole dept.
knew about this);   haircut in town . . . back to
the cottage.   Threatening to expose Donald
Gaylord? Did Donald follow him to the cottage?

2.   Helen Mann – revenge + jealousy. Lonely,
hoped to rekindle with Alan Sidebottom?
Slighted + rejected by him at the party. Jealous
of his celebrity status? Possibly gave up her only
child (+ now regrets it?), Sidebottom rebuffs
Helen publicly (party). Does a grown child of
Helen + Alan exist?

3. Mitchell Fender – jealously + revenge.
Plagiarism. Thinks Sidebottom ruined his career.
Mitchell's wife left him around same time.
Blames Sidebottom for everything. Makes a
huge show of patching things up with
Sidebottom, but is this just for show?
Mysterious illness. If Mitchell is dying, would
he feel he has nothing to lose and take revenge
on Sidebottom?

4. Donald Gaylord – fear of being outed by
Sidebottom and having his career ruined.
Protecting a double-life. Hugely ambitious,
wants to be Head of Dept. Could he and Sheila
Dubin be in cahoots? Does Donald suspect his
partner Jimmy of the murder?

5. Charlotte Cadell – revenge. Payback for
Sidebottom stealing her fiancé + ruining her life.

6. Nedda Cake – No real motive. Sidebottom plagiarized from Frank Cake's work decades ago. Ancient history.

7. Seth Dubin – revenge. Sidebottom humiliates him at the party. Embarrasses him in front of the whole dept. for his stammer. Sidebottom is Seth's hero. Did Sheila bully Seth into being her accomplice in getting revenge on Sidebottom? Doubtful.

8. Sheila Dubin – revenge. She has high hopes for Seth's career. When Sidebottom humiliates Seth at the party, Sheila vows revenge. In cahoots with Donald? Or is she possibly protecting Donald? Don't forget about her medical knowledge of poisons.

9. Jimmy Lopez – jealously? Does Jimmy think Donald is having an affair with Sidebottom? Or did Donald confide in Jimmy his worries about being outed by Sidebottom? Did Jimmy do Donald's dirty work, and get rid of Sidebottom?

Edwina stood back and looked at the board. Something bothered her about the list she had assembled, but she could not put her finger on what it was. There was no shortage of motive or opportunity . . . that wasn't exactly the problem . . . She reread what was written on the chalkboard from top to bottom, then from bottom to top.

Somehow this outline lacked *dimension.* All the players had a connection to the Department—that's what was bothering her.

This is a closed set, she thought. *What about Professor Sidebottom's life before his visit to New Guilford? It needs to be looked into.*

Wasn't it possible there was someone else who belonged on the list? She and Will had been assuming that Alan Sidebottom's murderer had to be someone connected to the college, to Sanborn House, but was that necessarily true?

Edwina recalled how at dinner that night at the Old World Tavern Professor Sidebottom had joked about being married more than once. That meant there could easily be neglected or vengeful ex-wives in the wings. And Helen Mann had made a remark about Professor Sidebottom being estranged from some or all of his children. Alan Sidebottom's children could easily be college-aged. What was to say one of them—or more than one—wasn't currently attending Cushing? Perhaps they killed him for the inheritance? And what was to say there weren't additional victims of plagiarism besides the ones Edwina knew about— Mitchell Fender and Nedda Cake's late husband? Maybe others had even tried to sue Sidebottom, and lost, as Mitchell Fender had. That could be a motive. Sidebottom was a wealthy man, and might stand to lose a lot of money if he lost a plagiarism suit. That made him a good target. What about Sidebottom's colleagues at Cambridge? The Distinguished Professor was known to be a serial philanderer. Just as an angry husband had come after Theodore Sanborn and shot him in the arm, maybe another angry husband had come after Sidebottom, and done a lot worse damage. Edwina could imagine a number of scenarios in which Professor Sidebottom's outré behavior might have pushed people too far.

Opening up the closed set of suspects to the wider world brought in a flood of new possibilities.

Edwina wrote on the chalkboard.

10. England. Ex-wives? (revenge, greed) Children? (greed) Legal altercations (plagiarism + other)? Colleagues? Girlfriends?

Before she left her office she flipped the chalkboard back to the other side, so her notes about the investigation would not be out in the open.

*

Over the course of the next few days, Edwina redoubled her investigative efforts, all the while managing to keep up with her academic duties, making sure she did not neglect preparing for class or any other matter related to school. She loved her job and understood what came first.

She set about looking into item # 10 from her chalkboard list, the investigation into Professor Sidebottom's connections back home in England. Beginning with Alan Sidebottom's colleagues, she sat at the computer and typed in Cambridge University, then went to the Physics and Astronomy Department page. From there she compiled a list of faculty members who comprised Professor Sidebottom's academic colleagues. Edwina painstakingly began researching these names one by one on the Internet, looking for anything in their biographical information that might hold significance or trigger another line of inquiry. She was keeping an eye out for legal imbroglios, messy divorce cases, custody battles. Later on, Edwina would cross-reference these faculty members against names of people from other walks of Alan Sidebottom's life—publishers, television producers, spouses, and children—and see if any sort of pattern emerged, if some names popped up repeatedly, or at least, more than others.

As for those ex-wives, girlfriends, and children, she was finding it a bit harder to glean details about them. Information about Alan Sidebottom's private life was harder to come by on the Internet because tittle-tattle makes no claim to be part of any particular professional province. You can't do a 'gossip' search. Edwina found any number of biographical sites listed for Professor Sidebottom, but they mostly dealt with his educational background, academic achievements and honors, and included very little in the way of personal information.

Gradually Edwina did manage to extract from various sites, with no great concern for reliability, a list of ex-wives and the children he had with them. Reliability was not the issue here; Edwina was willing to venture down as many rabbit holes as necessary in hopes of unearthing useful information.

Professor Sidebottom's bibliography was, of course, easy to access. There were many sites that listed his published credits, so Edwina had no problem gathering sites where she could find his articles. She would familiarize herself with them, so she could compare his writings against some of his colleagues' work, with an eye to sniffing out anything that might have been 'heavily borrowed'. She would add the names of people Professor Sidebottom had possibly plagiarized (if there were any) to her growing list. Likewise she would add the names of editors, publishers, and television producers he had worked with, and cross-reference all these names. Perhaps one or two names would emerge from the pack, and point Edwina in a useful direction.

This new leg of the investigation was time-consuming and tedious. It took days for Edwina to plow through all this new information, searching for connections that might have some bearing on Alan Sidebottom's death. Some small piece of information that seemed insignificant at first glance might redirect the inquiry onto a fresh path.

Edwina took a walk over to the main library at Hinley Hall, hoping to take out copies of Professor Sidebottom's three books. She wanted to re-acquaint herself with all his work, and perhaps get a clearer understanding of Mitchell Fender's claim of plagiarism.

Chapter 18

By the time Edwina got home Thursday evening she was feeling tired and hungry, and a little bit run down. She hadn't quite realized she had been working longer hours than usual, and getting less sleep because of all the time she was putting in on top of her regular workload—time spent on the Sidebottom investigation.

She took a hot bath and dressed in warm pajamas and a long, flannel robe. After dinner (grilled cheese, cucumber and tomato sandwich) she fed logs into the woodstove for the night, took vitamin C, and made a bourbon hot toddy. She padded upstairs and got into bed with Alan Sidebottom's books.

It had been years since she'd read them. She opened his extravagantly titled, *M Theory, My Arse!* and sipped hot toddy as she read. By the time she reached Chapter Three the hot toddy was gone. Halfway through the chapter, she was fast asleep with the book in her hands and the reading lamp on. Edwina slept straight through the night for twelve hours. She woke up the next morning at 7:30, ravenously hungry, and feeling much better than she had the night before.

Will texted her at eight o'clock

Anything interesting come up in your research? We are trying to get Jimmy Lopez's cell phone records, see if he traveled to NG, but no luck, yet.

Edwina texted back.

RU free 4 breakfast, Earls, 9:00?

*

Will was sitting at a corner table by the windows.

"I ordered chili and eggs for you. Is that okay?" he said.

"Fine," she said, getting out of her warm coat, hat and gloves, and laying them over the back of the chair. Her hair was static-y from the wool hat. A few blond hairs floated upwards toward the ceiling.

Earl set down a cup of tea for Edwina and coffee for Will.

"So, I thought it might be interesting to cross-reference some of the names I collected," Edwina began, shoving her bangs to the side. "You know—ex-wives, editors, children, work colleagues, stuff like that. I actually did get some interesting results, but nothing seemed very suspicious. Just gossipy stuff. Professor Sidebottom married the wife of a close friend. The man was also Sidebottom's book editor, and they continued working together, even after Sidebottom married the guy's wife. Then when the wife later left Sidebottom, she married one of his colleagues at Cambridge. I also discovered that Sidebottom's oldest son, Christopher, married one of his dad's ex-wives, who was close in age to Christopher. Jesus, how fraught can family relationships get? I was also reading through the records of the court case when Sidebottom was arrested for smashing up a bookstore window. Turns out it was a Scientology bookstore. Sidebottom was drunk at the time, but in court he said he would gladly do it again even if he was sober!"

Earl set down two orders of scrambled eggs with chili and cornbread. Edwina enthusiastically dug into her breakfast, pouring honey onto the cornbread and taking a big bite.

"Go on," prodded Will, enjoying Edwina's recitation. He dabbed at his chin with a napkin, signaling Edwina to do the same. A dab of honey trickled slowly toward the point of her heart-shaped face.

"Well," she said, scooping up a forkful of chili and eggs. "He once assaulted a prostitute, when he found out she was transgender. He would have gotten off with a charge of simple assault, but Sidebottom felt horrible about the whole thing and ended up paying her a lot of money."

"Then we have Rosamund Penrith-Godbold," Edwina continued. "Professor Sidebottom's third wife. There was a very nasty court case when they got divorced. She sued him for everything he had, including sole custody of their little daughter. But the court records say that during the trial Sidebottom exposed Rosamund for having had a string of affairs with women during their marriage, and he threatened to publish photos taken by a private investigator he hired, if Rosamund didn't back off. Sidebottom got shared custody of the little girl, and ended up not paying Rosamund much money. He called her an unfit mother. She attacked him in the courtroom. Physically."

"Wow," Will said. "Sounds like motive to me. But isn't she—"

"Nope, she's here in America," Edwina said. "She now lives with a painter in London, but the two of them have been in New York for an exhibition for the past two weeks."

"That's great. I'll check her out," said Will. "Anything else?"

Edwina asked for another cup of tea.

"Lots of stuff, but I think Rosamund's our best shot," she said.

After breakfast they lingered a few minutes outside Earl's, talking about the investigation.

"Where are you headed?" Will said.

"To school. I have a class."

"I was just wondering if you wanted to walk along the river a little bit?"

"Don't you have to get to work?" Edwina asked.

"I don't have to be in for a little while. Here, I'll take your bike," Will said, taking hold of Edwina's bike and walking it alongside him.

They strolled a few blocks north to Sycamore Street. At the end of Sycamore Street they headed down a small incline that lead to the River Walk, a public garden that meandered along the riverbank for the length of Main Street. The day was cold, but with no wind to chill them, Edwina and Will were enjoying the warmth of the bright sunshine.

Will received a text.

"My Chief says Jimmy Lopez's cell records are coming in this afternoon. That should be interesting," Will said.

"Do you think he's really a likely candidate for Professor Sidebottom's murder?" Edwina asked.

"I won't say he's at the top of my list, but it's a possibility. Jimmy Lopez would have had incredible ease of movement—nobody in New Guilford knows what he looks like, and he could have been in and out of here pretty quickly. Couples do each other's bidding all the time, and Gaylord could have put Jimmy up to it. He could have told Jimmy everything he needed to know about the layout of the Carriage House, where to park his car, and so on. It's even possible that Jimmy Lopez—or whoever killed Professor Sidebottom—was waiting for him outside the restaurant the night you had dinner with him. You said the whole Department knew the two of you would be at the Old World Tavern that night. Somebody could have stalked Sidebottom straight out of the restaurant until they had the opportunity to get the poison in him."

Will left Edwina at Sanborn House, then headed back to the police station, no more than a twenty-minute walk. As he strode across the Green along the campus path, Will was thinking about how Edwina's freckles were fading in the cold weather. He wondered if they'd be invisible by the time winter came.

*

A few days later Edwina was sitting in her office, marking exams, when she got a text from Will.

Rosamund Penrith is off the hook. Airtight alibi.
What about her partner? Edwina texted.
Checked that out, too. Both in the clear.

"Damn!" Edwina said aloud. "Back to the drawing board," she sighed.

None of the leads from her recent round of research were panning out. No secret Sidebottom offspring attended Cushing or appeared to live in the area. And the professor's misdemeanor offenses of public intoxication, assault, and vandalism hardly added up to someone wanting to kill him.

Edwina got up from the desk to stretch her legs. She approached the chalkboard, and flipped it to the reverse side, the side with her murder notes written on it, the side she was careful not to display when other people were in her office. As she stood reading it over, something bright pink across the room caught her eye.

She removed a pink flyer from on top of some books in the bookcase where she had absently placed it days earlier. Edwina studied the printed advertisement she held in her hands. It read, 'Leah's Place ~ A Hair Salon For Men & Women, Welcoming The College Community ~ First Visit 50% Off'. The ad included an address, phone number, and email address, and appeared in an attractive cursive font printed over a faintly reproduced botanical print showing old-fashioned style flowers in a bouquet. At the bottom of the page it said, 'Proprietor: Leah Block'.

Interesting name, Edwina thought. *Dutch, like Block Island.*

Edwina slowly gazed back up at the chalkboard, and looked again at the flyer in her hand. Something was trying to suggest itself to her, but she couldn't grasp it. Was it something about the flyer? Was it a connection between the flyer and what was written on the chalkboard? She examined them both over and over again, searching for a spark of an idea. She could faintly sense that a connection was trying to forge itself in the back of her mind, a triangle connecting some part of the information on the chalkboard and something written on the sheet of pink paper, and Alan Sidebottom's death. She just couldn't work out what it was.

Edwina had a class to teach. She gathered up a pile of exams and loaded them into her backpack. She set off for the new classroom building across the Green.

"I'm handing back your exams today," she said, making her way around the classroom, distributing papers. "I want to let you know that I enjoyed reading them. They showed a good grasp of the concepts we've been talking about. Today I want to go over some of the more difficult ideas, the ones many of you are finding hard to understand. We all need to get on the same page." She stopped in front of Dylan D'Arcy.

"Here you go, Dylan," she said, handing the young man his exam. "Very creative. I especially enjoyed the anagram you made out of 'critical hypotheses— 'hypothetical crises'? Nice touch," she chuckled.

Students were busily flipping through the pages of their exams, comparing grades, reading Edwina's remarks, and commiserating among themselves. Edwina made her way back to the front of the classroom.

"Okay, let's put them away for now. We will go over the exams later, I promise," she said. "But for right now, let's talk about some of the trickier aspects involved in the optical properties of solids."

When the commotion of rustling papers and chatter died down, Edwina held court to a very attentive audience.

*

After class Edwina strolled across the Green toward Sanborn House at a leisurely pace, enjoying the fresh air and the sunshine. She thought about Dylan D'Arcy's clever anagram and smiled. By the time she got back to her office, her thoughts had once again returned to the Sidebottom business. Edwina picked up the pink flyer and examined it carefully.

There was really nothing strange or unusual about it. It was a discount flyer, like so many others, that came in the mail.

Oh, but wait a second. This didn't come in the mail. Ruth Benjamin said they were hand-delivered, Edwina thought. *Okay. So what might that signify?*

Edwina hung up her jacket on the door. She stood at the window and looked out at the superb fall colors.

Some of the trees had lost their leaves. Winter was around the corner. A New England winter, at that.

Because whoever mailed them wanted to leave nothing to chance, Edwina postulated. *Because whoever delivered them to the Department wanted to make absolutely sure they got here in a nice, neat pile, and weren't thrown out by some overzealous department secretary sorting the mail.*

Edwina sat at her desk and began to write an outline for her lecture on the Gaussian distribution formula. But her student, Dylan D'Arcy, kept popping into her head unexpectedly, and interrupting her train of thought.

How incredibly annoying, Edwina thought. *Why in the world would—*

Edwina snatched up the pink flyer and studied the image of fairy fingers in the background, with text in the foreground. She grabbed the phone and dialed Will. The call went straight to voice mail. She hurriedly punched out a text message.

No reply.

Wait 'til you hear back from Will. Don't do anything silly, she thought.

Impossible! Once the discovery had been made, there was no real chance of Edwina slowing down. A cousin to her 'premature absent-mindedness' was this compulsion to pursue any piece of evidence that presented itself on the way to a solution, no matter how reckless it might prove.

It did cross her mind that she might be putting herself in harm's way, but she quickly pushed this thought out of the equation. A new connection had presented itself, and she would follow it, with or without Will. No time to waste!

Edwina jammed the pink flyer into her backpack, flew down the stairs, and jumped on her bike. The day was raw and damp. Her ears, face, and hands instantly stung from the bitter cold. Her nose started to run. Pedaling hard and squinting her eyes against the cold, she pulled the hat back out of her jacket pocket, and maneuvered it awkwardly onto her head in a lopsided position that at least did manage to cover her ears. From the other pocket she extracted the gloves. Pedaling furiously, she held one glove in her teeth while she wriggled the other glove onto her right hand.

"Dammit!" Edwina cursed, speeding past the second glove as it fell to the ground in a red blur.

She tugged at the left sleeve of her coat, trying to coax it as far over her bare hand as she could in order to keep her fingers from freezing. That didn't work, so she stuck her bare hand into the pocket of her coat and steered the bike with the other.

Almost there! Edwina thought, seeing the opening of the alley a hundred yards ahead.

Edwina got off her bike. She paused to catch her breath, and wiped her nose on a tissue. She peered down the length of the alley, lined with trim little whitewashed storefronts, looking inviting with their matching awnings and colorful flowerboxes.

Edwina got a fix on Leah's Place.

Okay, kid, what's the plan? she thought excitedly.

Edwina locked up her bike and strolled casually as possible down the alley toward Leah's Place. She nervously entered the salon.

Leah looked up from behind a desk.

"Hello," Leah said politely. "Can I help you?"

"Hi," Edwina said. "I'm sorry I don't have an appointment, but I was wondering if you could possibly fit me in for a trim? Just the bangs?" Edwina said, brushing them out of her eyes for emphasis.

"Oh sure, no problem! Why don't you go in the back and get a smock on," she said, taking the measure of Edwina with a covert glance from head to toe.

Edwina hung her jacket on coat hooks near the door, and surveyed the airy salon. A muted whir of washing machines from the Laundromat next door hummed pleasantly in the background. The walls of the small salon were painted a tranquil shade of pink, and botanical prints in white wooden frames decorated the walls. Rectangular mirrors, also framed in white wood, hung at two, well-appointed styling stations sitting side by side. Stacks of neatly folded pink towels lined the shelves of a wrought iron and brass baker's rack. The pale linoleum floor did not betray a speck of dust.

Edwina approached the back of the salon where a hallway led to a small changing room. She took down a smock from a hook on the back of the changing room door, and snapped it closed over her shirt. On her way out she peered into the little bathroom across the hall, with sparkling white tiled walls and floor that smelled of lavender. A skylight was cranked opened for ventilation in the immaculate little powder pink bathroom. The entire salon was spotless.

Edwina sat down in an imitation leather and chrome chair at the haircutting station nearer the front door.

Leah stood behind her and addressed Edwina's reflection in the mirror.

"So, just a little bit off the bangs?" she asked cheerfully.

"Yes, please," Edwina replied. "An inch would be good. Seems like my bangs are always getting in my eyes."

Leah combed Edwina's hair with expertly brisk strokes, and gathered it into a neat twist. She secured the twist of hair with a clip, leaving only the bangs free.

"You have beautiful hair," Leah said. "Very healthy."

"Thank-you."

Leah reached over and removed a black nylon cape from the lower shelf of the workstation. In one fluid motion, she shook it open and encircled Edwina' body with the voluminous garment. The billowy 'cutting cape' fluttered into place and covered Edwina's body, all the way down to her knees. Leah snapped it closed at the back of Edwina's neck. The 'cutting cape' provided a protective layer, and ensured against chemical hair product and hair falling onto Edwina's skin or clothing.

"So, are you a student up at the college?" Leah asked, combing Edwina's hair.

"Actually, I teach there."

"That must be really interesting. What do you teach?"

"Physics," Edwina replied.

"Oh, wow, so you must've known that poor man who got killed," Leah said.

"It was horrible. Such a nice man. And brilliant. I had dinner with him the night he got killed. It's so weird that he came here for a haircut after we had dinner together."

"Boy, oh boy, what a small world," Leah said. "Were you his girlfriend or something?"

"Oh, no, nothing like that," Edwina said. "Speaking of physics, I noticed that your name is an anagram for 'black hole'."

"No kidding?" Leah said. "How about that?"

Leah had nearly finished cutting Edwina's bangs in a perfectly straight line.

"If you went out to dinner with him, it must have been like a date," Leah said. "I mean, you're a beautiful girl, and he was a horny, old fraud."

There was an abrupt change in the atmosphere with this alarmingly inappropriate comment. Menace was afoot.

Suddenly Leah grabbed the sides of the capacious nylon garment covering Edwina, and pulled it tightly across Edwina's body, trapping her in the chair. Leah tied the cape behind the chair, knotting it firmly, so that it was like a straightjacket. Edwina could move only her legs. Leah grabbed another cape from the shelf, and tied Edwina's thighs together so she wouldn't be able to kick her. The strong nylon fabric made an effective restraint.

Leah removed the clip holding Edwina's hair in a twist, and let it fall in loose waves around Edwina's neck. Adrenaline flooded Edwina's brain and triggered a strong desire for flight. She wriggled her body, but she was firmly tied to the chair. The nylon capes were as strong as rope. Edwina's stomach felt like it was rising to her mouth, and her mind reeled. Her heart pounded so loudly she could not hear, and wondered if she had gone deaf.

"What do you think you're doing?" Edwina shouted, terrified.

A coldly menacing smile transformed Leah's face into something grotesque.

"You must think I was born on a farm, if you think I'm going to let myself get caught by the likes of you." Leah threw her head of dark hair back and laughed hysterically.

"The hilarious thing is that you would be so fucking right—I *was* born on a farm! Born and raised! I'm the real deal—I'm Dorothy from Kansas! Believe me— cows and chickens and pig shit and the whole stinking, mind-numbing thing," Leah gabbled, clicking together a pair of scissors rapidly next to Edwina's ear.

Leah took slow, deliberate steps around the chair until she was standing facing Edwina. She moved slowly closer to her with the scissors and began randomly hacking off chunks of hair.

"Why the name 'Leah Block'," Edwina sputtered, trying to stall Leah from chopping off all her hair—or worse. "Why the subterfuge by picking a name that spells out 'black hole'?"

Leah held the scissors in mid-air.

"Clever, right? I just thought the name was a clever touch—I wanted to make sure everybody knew how smart I am. And if it got their attention, all the better."

"Whose attention?" Edwina gasped.

"Sidebottom, and his gal Friday, Helen Mann."

"Why them?"

Leah posed in an exaggerated stance of mock exasperation, her hand on her hips and eyes wide.

"Are you telling me you don't see the family resemblance?" Leah said. *Really,* Nancy Drew? God! You nerds are morons! They're my *parents,* Goldilocks! And just as soon as I finish my business with Helen Mann, better known to me as dear old Mom, I can't wait to leave this place."

Suddenly Edwina's mind quieted down, and her heart slowed to normal. She no longer felt panicked. She felt angry. Her mind was now sharply focused. She looked hard into Leah's eyes.

"So, what did Alan Sidebottom ever do to you?" Edwina said calmly.

Leah glared at her. She inched slowly closer with scissors in hand. Edwina told herself not to wriggle or make any sudden movement, as this was likely to end up disastrously for her. She forced herself to sit very still when she felt the cold metal of the scissors against her forehead, and Leah began to cut her hair shorter and shorter. Edwina was afraid to close her eyes, and afraid to keep them open.

Neither spoke as Leah pranced around the chair, cutting random hunks of Edwina's hair. Edwina's view was blocked from seeing her reflection in the mirror, but she could see thick, uneven sections of hair falling to the floor. She started to feel sick.

Focus on getting out of here, she cajoled herself. *Think!*

The heavy salon chair sat on a round metal base that spun in both directions. She could move only her legs, from the knees down. Edwina calculated that she might be able to knock Leah off balance by spinning the chair hard enough, and banging into Leah with the metal footrest that stuck out at the bottom of the chair. She would have to spin the chair with maximum force if she was going to knock Leah off balance.

Edwina waited for the right moment. She quietly positioned her feet to one side so she could push off the floor at an angle, and spin the chair with adequate force. She could not think beyond that.

Edwina did not have time to give the matter further consideration. Leah suddenly moved in very close. She grabbed a fistful of hair on top of Edwina's head and yanked it straight up. She chopped it off in one snip. Edwina seized the moment. She steadied her feet, and pushed off the floor as hard as she could. The chair spun rapidly around, hitting Leah's legs with the metal footrest.

Leah cried out. She stumbled backwards. A hand mirror and hair dryer clattered to the floor with a crash. Edwina knew this was far from a debilitating blow, and that she had no time to lose if she wanted to escape. She struggled to her feet, and hobbled as awkwardly as imaginable, with a chair tied to her back, toward the front door. Turning sideways to protect her head and face, Edwina crashed into the front door, shattering the panel of glass. She flung herself through the opening, hoping to land with the back of the chair hitting the ground first. In this way she would be at least slightly buffered from the impact, and her head would be less likely to crack open like a coconut.   As she flew through the clattering glass she hoped someone inside the Laundromat, or other passer-by, would hear the commotion and come to her aid.

192 PHYSICS CAN BE FATAL

Chapter 19

When Edwina's eyes opened at last she tried to focus on a blurry object that appeared to be green and yellow. Her body throbbed with pain, and she had a brutal headache. Gradually, yellow roses came into focus. Edwina wondered where she was.

Slowly she turned her head and a figure appeared nearby.

"How you feeling?"

Edwina grinned. She tried to speak but her lips were so dry they stuck together. The person in the room held up a glass of water for her to sip.

"Hi, Will," Edwina croaked.

Her face and head were bruised and cut, and she had two black eyes. Remarkably there were no broken bones, but one side of her body was badly bruised, and there were cuts and lacerations on her arms and legs and hands.

"Nice haircut," said a voice from the corner.

Nedda Cake was sitting quietly in a chair by the window. She rose and walked toward Edwina, and perched on the side of the bed.

"Baked you some shortbread," the old professor said, tapping on a tin box she held in her lap. "You had everybody in the department worried sick, you know."

"What happened?" Edwina said, extending a hand gingerly to her bruised head and feeling her hair, which had been chopped short and lopsided.

"You went to see Leah Block at her salon. Do you remember that?" Will said solicitously. "Later, when you're feeling better, you'll have to explain to me why you went to see her."

"Sure," Edwina said closing her eyes. "I remember she tied me to a chair. I thought she was going to kill me. I think I remember jumping through a glass door."

"You should probably use a stunt double for stuff like that in future," Will said.

A doctor with a kind face and a calm demeanor entered the room. She extended her hand toward Edwina.

"I'm Dr. Kurra," she said, smiling. "How are you feeling?"

"Not too bad," Edwina said, struggling to sit up. "Ow. My head," she moaned, sliding back down in the bed.

"You will be pretty sore for some weeks," Dr. Kurra said. "Your body is badly bruised, but luckily, your concussion was not too serious. It's lucky you were tied to that chair because it acted like a seat belt. Otherwise, you would have been thrown from the vehicle, so to speak, and would have sustained far worse injuries. There are no broken bones, just bruising and a few cuts. Nothing very deep. Your body is going to turn some amazing colors, but don't let it worry you. Those are the colors of healing. Unfortunately, there's nothing I can do about the haircut," Dr. Kurra smiled.

Edwina laughed for the first time since the accident.

"Thank-you for everything, doctor. When can I go home?" Edwina said.

"You know, it's funny. Your friends here predicted you would ask me that," Dr. Kurra chuckled. "I would like you to stay one more night. You can go home in the morning."

Will picked Edwina up at the hospital the following morning. They stopped for groceries on the way to her house.

"Do you have anybody who can stay with you for a few days, until you get your strength back?" Will asked, putting away the groceries.

"I'll be fine," Edwina said, filling the kettle with water. "It's really not necessary. I'm feeling much better already."

Will wanted to tell Edwina he was worried that Leah Block might come after her. She had tried to harm Edwina once, and she might try again. But he decided against confiding these fears in Edwina. They would only alarm her, and maybe he was overreacting. Besides, Leah Block was nowhere to be found, and had most likely hightailed it out of New Guilford.

They sat at the kitchen table having tea and blueberry muffins from Dan's Bridge Market Bakery.

"So tell me the whole thing," Edwina said, cautiously biting into a warm muffin.

"First of all, let me just say that I'm glad you're okay. It could have been a whole lot worse. You know that, right?" Will said.

Edwina nodded; crumbs fell onto her shirt.

"And I swore I wouldn't do this, but—I did tell you not to snoop around on your own. I hate to say 'I told you so', but you really need to stop doing things like that."

Edwina nodded again. Will stirred honey into his tea and drank some.

"You were lucky," he began. "There was a Cushing student doing laundry next door at the Laundromat. While her clothes were in the dryer she walked next door to see if she could get a haircut. There was a 'Closed' sign on the door, but when she peered in, she could see you in the chair and Leah cutting your hair. She watched for long enough to see that something wasn't right, and she called the cops."

Will took another drink of tea.

"We arrived minutes after you crashed through the front door, and the ambulance raced you to the hospital. The student waited with you until the ambulance arrived, but she never saw Leah leave the salon. When we rushed in to arrest her, she was nowhere to be seen. She had crawled out of a skylight in the bathroom and jumped in her car."

Edwina was feeling sleepy and her headache was starting to come back.

"Wow, I need to thank that student. You have her name, right? But right now I'm kind of tired. I think I'd better go upstairs and lie down."

Will walked upstairs with Edwina. She nudged off her shoes and fell quickly to sleep. Will covered her with the quilt at the foot of the bed and closed the door to her bedroom.

He felt uneasy about leaving Edwina alone in the house, so he hung around downstairs, tidying up, rinsing out the cups and plates. He checked in with Chief Burnstein and she okayed him to stay at Edwina's house for as long as he deemed necessary.

He looked around for something to do. The fire needed stoking, and he added a few more logs. Will put the fresh eggs on the counter in a bowl, and burned the paper egg carton in the woodstove.

He wandered through the little house. A center hall staircase divided the living room on one side and the kitchen on the other. The dining room had been incorporated into the kitchen years earlier. It was obvious from the sparse furnishings in the living room that Edwina did not use it much. A sofa and chairs arranged on a hooked rug sat in front of a fireplace that looked as if it hadn't had a fire burning in it for some time. There was a pair of owl-figured andirons, with large eye-holes for flickering flames to show through, but there were no ashes in the firebox. Open muslin curtains on metal rods framed the windows. A handsome mantle clock carved with wood scrolls sat over the fireplace.

Will came back into the kitchen, still poking around for something to busy himself with while Edwina slept. He stood at the back wall of the kitchen gazing out the windows. His project suddenly appeared. The paving stones in Edwina's terrace had not been properly laid, and the changing temperatures from winter to summer had caused them to heave out of place. Will would remove them, dig a proper foundation, and replace them so they would no longer shift around.

First order of business was to find something for digging. Will put on his coat and gloves, and walked out to a utility shed in the back. Along with the cobwebs and mice nests there was a decent collection of tools hanging on hooks. He grabbed a spade and a shovel.

Will removed the slate slabs from the ground and set them aside. They were not especially thick, and he figured digging out two inches of dirt would provide a stable foundation for the terrace. Thankfully, the dirt was not too hard. In another month the ground would have been frozen, and impossible to dig.

Will retrieved the wheelbarrow from the shed, and wheeled it to the gravel driveway of Edwina's house. He shoveled gravel into the wheelbarrow until it was full. He returned to the construction site and dumped the gravel into the newly dug footprint of the terrace. He used a rake to spread the gravel all around. Now the fun part came, putting the slate pavers back together in a pleasing and efficient configuration as possible.

When he was finally finished, Will sat on a tree stump to assess the job he had done.

Not bad, he thought.

Will returned everything to the shed and cleaned up the work site before he went back in the house to wash up and find something to eat. Edwina appeared in the kitchen doorway, having slept for three hours, just as Will was biting into his second blueberry muffin.

"Oh, hi," she said, surprised to find Will still there.

"I hope you don't mind me hanging around. I just wanted to make sure you were okay before I took off."

"No, it's fine. Thanks."

Edwina made a pot of tea and invited Will to stay. She knew he was eager to talk about the recent turn the investigation had taken. They sat down at the kitchen table.

"Are you sure you feel up to talking?" Will asked.

"I'm fine, Will," she said, sipping tea. "Remember my idea about Professor Sidebottom and Helen Mann possibly having had a child?" she began. "It was Professor Cake who put the idea in my head. Over the years I have learned that she generally says things for a specific reason, and that's why I wasn't willing to let go of the idea. Professor Cake can be wily—sometimes even oblique—and it kept coming back to me that she went out of her way to point me in the direction of a baby. I thought I had pursued it as far as I could. But I was wrong."

Will listened intently as Edwina continued.

"You told me when you went to the Carriage House you noticed a smell in the bedroom you described as a sweet chemical, or something like that, right? Nowhere else, but in the bedroom? And specifically, the bed, right?"

"Right."

"Then it turned out Professor Sidebottom used one of these when he got a haircut on the last night of his life," Edwina said, reaching across the table for her backpack.

"Everybody in the department got one of these, you know," she said, pulling out the flyer. "I would bet the Physics Department is probably the only place that received them. I think we were targeted by this salon— specifically, Alan Sidebottom. And Helen Mann."

"Take a closer look at it," Edwina said.

Edwina laid the sheet of pink paper on the table where she and Will could examine it together. She ran her finger slowly down the page to the bottom.

"'Proprietor Leah Block'," she read out loud. "Move the letters of her name around."

Will studied the name on the flyer. Edwina handed him a pencil.

"Black hole?" he said.

"Kind of a strange coincidence, isn't it? You do realize black holes are incredibly significant in the physics and astronomy community. They're pretty much the holy grail," Edwina said. "I think she did it to get people's attention, hoping it would lure them in. As it happened, Professor Sidebottom went there because it was the only place open at night."

Will studied Edwina intently as he processed these new details in the case.

"And I think I know what the smell was at the Carriage House," she continued. "I smell it every time I get a hair cut. It's the smell of hair salons. It's the mixture of chemicals and sweet-smelling additives they put in to mask the acrid smell. Stuff like propylene and dimethicone. Chemicals used in hair conditioners. I think our killer poisoned Professor Sidebottom by adding in a chemical of her own, something that would trigger a heart attack. I think she mixed the poison in with a heavy dose of shampoo and conditioner. She probably had a special little bottle of it at the ready, hidden away, waiting and hoping Alan Sidebottom or Helen Mann would show up for a haircut one day. She would have worn gloves to massage it into his scalp. The poison would have worked its way into his system, and then it was just a matter of time until lights out."

"And why would she want to kill Alan Sidebottom or Helen Mann?"

"Remember the conference in Brussels where Professor Sidebottom and Helen met? Do the math, Will. Leah Block is their daughter. Their crazy, vengeful, daughter."

Chapter 20

The forensic unit discovered a minute amount of poisonous substance on a hand towel inside the salon. The towels had all been laundered, but astonishingly, a tiny trace of the deadly mixture had remained behind on one fluffy, pale pink hand towel.

Chief Burnstein contacted the police and FBI in New York City. It took them a week to find Leah Block. She had dyed her hair blond, and was hiding out in a friend's apartment from the last salon where she had worked. They arrested her on suspicion of murder, and drove her back to New Guilford.

Will and Chief Valerie Burnstein were finally sitting across a table from Leah Block in an interview room at the New Guilford Police Station.

Their suspect, whose real (adopted) name was Penny Crawford, seemed largely unconcerned by her arrest for the murder of Alan Sidebottom. If anything, she relished the attention.

"I'm sure my mother, once she learns of my existence, will fly to my aid. We'll probably become very close, you know. She must have missed me terribly all these years," Penny sneered. "She can hardly allow her only child in all the world to go to prison. Think of the publicity for good, old Cushing."

"So your birth mother, Helen Mann, knew nothing of your presence in New Guilford?" asked Will.

"She knows nothing of me at all, except that she tossed me out like last year's fashion thirty-three years ago. What a delightful surprise all this should make," Penny said. "Kind of an early Christmas present."

"Why the name 'Leah Block'?" Chief Val asked.

A hateful expression crept over Penny's face. Her long mouth twisted into a baleful grin.

"Why not?" she said. "I came into this world from a black hole. So did you. And we'll all disappear into the eternal misery of a black hole some day. All of life eventually goes the way of black holes. There's simply no getting away from them."

Will was trying to get the measure of this strange personality Penny Crawford presented, so different from when he interviewed her in the salon. She had seemed friendly, and cooperative, and *normal* then. In the interview room her demeanor slithered from resentful to coy to threatening, and back again in an instant.

"You're a clever girl," Chief Val said. "You obviously inherited your parents' brainpower."

"So true. Wouldn't they be proud of me?" Penny deadpanned.

"Would you like to tell us how you came up with your plan?" Chief Val asked.

"I thought you'd never ask," Penny said.

She shifted in her chair and asked for a glass of water.

"I did a search and found out who my birth mother was a few months ago, when I was feeling at loose ends, and finding myself in need of a substantial cash infusion and a change of scenery," Penny said. "It was time for me to try my luck elsewhere, so I moved up here to the green pastures of New Guilford," she said. "All this fresh air does a girl a lot of good."

Chief Val and Will remained quiet, wishing to reinforce Penny's feeling that the spotlight was all hers, for as long as she wanted it.

"I tried to find out about my birth father, but he wasn't listed in the birth records, so I began looking into Helen Mann's background. I learned she had been at a physics symposium in Brussels the summer I would have been conceived. Naughty, naughty Helen."

Penny paused to take a sip of water. She shot a wink at Will.

"I was able to find a list of academics who attended the symposium, but that's as close as I could get to figuring out who my father was."

"Then, when I read in the wonderfully quaint college newspaper about the famous Professor Alan Sidebottom coming to teach at Cushing this semester, I remembered his name from the list at the symposium. I figured it couldn't be a coincidence." She locked eyes with Chief Val with an expression of self-satisfied superiority.

"When I saw a picture of him on the Internet, I knew for sure. The resemblance between us is pretty striking, wouldn't you say? And then when I started to read about him, I found out he was not only famous, but stinking rich, and not only stinking rich, but estranged from his kids and ex-wives. What a tragedy. I figured I had a good shot at some money. So I wrote to him, explaining who I was, and asked for money. He wrote back a very rude and angry letter, basically telling me to piss off. That made me mad. That made me extremely mad, because I felt he really owed me, you know? That's when I hatched a plan to lure him into the salon."

"How do you mean, he 'owed' you?" Chief Val asked.

Penny regarded Val with a cold stare.

"What could you possibly not understand about that statement?" Penny asked.

"Did you mean he owed you in terms of money, or attention, or time, or . . .?" Chief Val answered calmly.

"My dear Mrs. Small-town-Chief-of-Police, it should be obvious even to you that he owed me all of those things," Penny said slowly and distinctly, as if to someone who was just learning to speak English.

"Back to my story," Leah continued. "I was overjoyed that night when he stumbled into my salon. Really, I could hardly believe it. Unfortunately for him, he not notice the obvious resemblance between us, and he made a pass at me. That was it. He had to go. Right then, right there."

"Why didn't you leave New Guilford after you killed Professor Sidebottom?" asked Chief Val. "You must have worried about getting caught?"

Penny Crawford laughed.

"What, me worry? Besides, the score was only one down and one to go. I'm a very patient girl, you know. I was just biding my time 'til I came up with a plan to get money out of that old whore of a mother. If Dad wouldn't give me my allowance, I sure wasn't going to leave town until I got it from Mom."

"One thing about me you really should know," Penny continued, "is that I don't like being ignored. I really don't like it. You might want to remember that, big guy," she said to Will, uncrossing and re-crossing her legs.

"Were you a hairdresser in New York?" Chief Val asked.

"Funny thing about that. The clientele can be so finicky," Penny said," always complaining to my bosses about me, for no good reason whatsoever. Just a lot of blather from a bunch of rich Park Avenue bitches, pardon my French. Eventually all the salons had to let me go, just to satisfy the customers."

"So, you set up shop in New Guilford, and sent out flyers to the Physics Department?" Will said.

"Yes, indeedy. I had seen a recent photo of Papa Sidebottom. He looked absurd with that ridiculous hair of his. I figured by offering a fifty percent discount, I had a chance of reeling him in—English people are so cheap, you know? I was going to make it seventy-five percent, but I thought that might look suspicious. As I say, I could not believe my luck when he showed up that night. I was all ready to be patient and wait it out, but like a moth to the flame—voilá—he came. And the rest, as they say, is misery!"

"How did you know about that particular poison?" Chief Val asked.

"Elementary, my dear Watson!" Penny said. "I was raised by a, rather dull, extremely fat woman named Betty, and her even duller husband, Hank. Betty taught me all sorts of useful things on the farm, like how to grow vegetables and flowers—some of them poisonous—how to milk cows and kill chickens—all sorts of neat stuff."

"But, alas, I'm a city girl at heart, and the bright lights beckoned me away from our idyllic life on the farm," she added, suddenly bursting into the first few bars of *Somewhere Over The Rainbow.*

Chief Val and Will waited, stone faced, for her to finish.

"When you were with Alan Sidebottom at the salon, why didn't you tell him who you were?" Chief Val asked.

Penny grinned.

"Oh, I wanted to—in fact, I was dying to—but I decided against it. I was afraid it might scare him away if I confessed my true identity, and then I wouldn't be able to do my magic. The folks back on the farm would have been so proud of me. I remembered to wear gloves so the poison wouldn't get all over me."

"Are you absolutely sure you wish to continue this interview without a lawyer?" Will said.

"Oh, I wouldn't worry about it, sport," Penny laughed. "I expect Mom can afford the best defense lawyer around."

Chapter 21

On the way downstairs to afternoon tea, Edwina knocked on Mitchell Fender's door.

"Come in!"

"Hi, Mitchell, do you have a minute?"

"Sure. Come in. Sit down, Edwina," Mitchell said affably.

Edwina sat uncomfortably for a moment, fidgeting, unsure how to begin.

"I owe you an apology, Mitchell," she started.

"Is that so?" Mitchell said. "What for?"

"I got a little carried away with all of this Alan Sidebottom business—you know—with the investigation and everything."

"Looks like you made a darn good job of it," Mitchell said.

"The thing is, I was riding my bike one morning and I saw you and Nedda going into the clinic. I don't know what possessed me—my curiosity got the better of me, I guess. I went into the clinic and said I was your niece, just so I could find out what you were doing there."

Mitchell sat silently for a moment.

"What did you find out?" he said.

"That you were seeing a neurologist, Dr. Elizabeth Swisher."

"What else?"

"That's it." Edwina looked down at her lap.

"I guess you'd like to know what I was doing there?" Mitchell said.

"Oh, no! You don't owe me an explanation, Mitchell. I feel terrible about snooping like that, and I just hope you're not angry with me. It goes without saying, I hope your situation isn't serious, and if there's ever anything I can do to help, I'll do it."

"Thank-you, Edwina. That's very kind," Mitchell said softly.

"As it happens," he continued, "I have a benign brain tumor. The doctor seems to feel comfortable keeping an eye on it for now, so nothing has to be done for the time being," he said.

"Thank goodness it's benign," Edwina gushed.

"Yup. I'm just trying to keep my mind on other things. No good dwelling on it, and no use worrying too much," Mitchell said, trying to disabuse himself of worry. "Things will work themselves out, one way or another."

For a few moments the only sound in the office was the watery tinkle of bamboo wind chimes near the open window.

"Let's go down to tea, shall we?" Edwina said. "Being around friends is always the best thing."

*

Word got around fast that it was Edwina who had cracked the case. She was the center of attention at tea that afternoon, besieged for details by everyone. Only Helen Mann was absent.

Refreshments in hand, students and teachers gathered around Edwina, until the entire department was crowded into one corner of the library. The air of suspicion that had draped itself over Sanborn House since Alan Sidebottom's death soon evaporated into the air with the clinking of china cups and saucers, and the *bonhomie.*

"Well done, Edwina," said Seth Dubin, perched on an ottoman, his teacup raised in a toast.

"Hear, hear!" everyone shouted.

"I hate to tell you this," Edwina laughed, sitting on a sofa between Nedda Cake and Mitchell Fender. Her jaggedly chopped hair looked awful, and she still had plenty of bruises and cuts on her face. "But we all fell under suspicion at the beginning. Then Nedda put the idea in my head that Professor Sidebottom and Helen might have had a child together—"

"Wild, unsubstantiated, guesswork," Nedda interjected. "Some of my best work."

"And a bunch of you are in the right age range to be their love child," Edwina continued. "The idea being, that a long-lost child of Alan Sidebottom and Helen might be motivated by revenge or greed, or some dastardly thing like that."

"So this girl came to New Guilford with a plan to kill Alan? How'd she know he would even be in New Guilford?" asked Donald Gaylord.

"She didn't," Edwina said. "She had been living in New York, working as a hairdresser, when she wasn't getting fired. She was in and out of money troubles and trouble with the police. One day she got the bright idea to do some research and find out who her birth parents were. She found out Helen was her birth mother, and decided to come up here and try to get money out of her somehow, by hook or by crook. But the father was unlisted on the birth records, so she didn't know who he was. She opened the salon in New Guilford, sent those pink flyers to the department, and waited, hoping Helen would show up."

"What was she going to do if Helen never came into the salon?" Lois Lieberman said.

"I don't think she thought it through that far. She's obviously crazy, and I think she made up her plan more or less as she went along," Edwina said. "I think eventually she would have shown up at the Department and confronted Helen in person. Maybe even blackmailed her. God knows."

"How did she even know about Alan Sidebottom?" Mitchell Fender said.

"Poor Professor Sidebottom. It was rotten luck," Edwina said.

"Penny Crawford," Edwina continued, "that's her actual name, happened to read in the college paper about Professor Sidebottom coming to Cushing this semester. She had already figured out—where would we be without the Internet?—that Helen had been in Brussels the summer Penny was conceived. Penny recognized Alan Sidebottom's name from the list of attendees at the Brussels conference, saw a picture of him and noticed her resemblance to him, and put two and two together. She wrote to him asking for money, and he completely blew her off. Then, when he showed up at the salon, she was furious that he didn't notice the resemblance between them. Then he made the fatal mistake of making a pass at her. That sealed his fate, and she decided to poison him right then."

Edwina took a sip of tea. The library was silent for a few moments, except for the ticking of the clock on the mantle.

"Will Tenney—the detective—says Penny Crawford has huge issues with men, with being abandoned and ill-treated, and so on. I think she figured Professor Sidebottom deserved the punishment of death for refusing to give her money, for ignoring her, for denying her very existence—for blowing her off at every turn. But the truth is probably that Professor

Sidebottom didn't even know Helen had his baby all those years ago."

"Then we come to the poison. This was truly diabolical. I was staring at that pink flyer she sent everyone. Remember how it had a background design of an old botanical print? I finally remembered where I had seen that same kind of flower before. The night I had dinner at The New World with Professor Sidebottom, he was admiring the murals. He told me a story about a cat he had as a boy that died from eating flowers just like ones in the mural. Tall, spikey, purple flowers. I looked them up and made the connection: they were the same flowers on Penny Crawford's flyer. Foxgloves. Latin name: *digitalis purpurea.* If you grind up the flower you get digoxin, the same ingredient that's in Professor Sidebottom's heart medication. Only, if you take a huge dose of it, it will trigger a massive heart attack. Penny mixed some in with shampoo or conditioner, or both, and rubbed it into Sidebottom's scalp. Later that night, when he was asleep, he had a fatal heart attack."

"How would she even know about such a thing?" asked Ravi Kapoor.

"All gardeners know about it," said Paolo Rossetti. "It's the reason a lot of people don't grow foxglove in their garden. Dangerous to pets."

"Penny Crawford grew up on a farm in the Midwest. She knew a lot about plants and things," Edwina said. "She knew all she had to do was to introduce a large amount of digoxin into his blood stream. It was easy to mix it in with whatever hair products she used on him. Don't forget, Professor Sidebottom was drunk at the salon. Penny told Will Tenney that he even dozed off at the sink. She could have been massaging the poison into his head for ten or twenty minutes, if he was asleep. That would be plenty long enough to get it into his bloodstream."

"How incredibly cruel," Charlotte Cadell said.

"It's inhuman," Seth Dubin said, shaking his head. "Wicked beyond measure."

"I wonder if she thought she would get away with it?" Donald Gaylord said.

"It's really pretty clever," Lois Lieberman said. "She actually might have gotten away with it, if it hadn't been for our very own Miss Marple, here."

"What about Helen?" Donald asked. "Was this wicked girl going to murder her, too?"

"No idea," Edwina said. "It probably depended on Penny's whims. Maybe Helen would have come to harm if she didn't shell out serious money. I don't know."

The library fell silent over the thought of Helen's narrow escape from death.

"I feel that Professor Sanborn should be here for this," Charlotte Cadell announced.

Ravi Kapoor jumped to his feet.

"I will help you fetch him!" he exclaimed, eager to assist.

Charlotte and Ravi reappeared a few minutes later, wheeling Theodore Sanborn into the library in his glass case, and parked him squarely amidst the group.

Donald Gaylord brought down an excellent bottle of Port from his office. Charlotte Cadell got paper cups from the kitchen, filled them with Donald's Port and passed them around.

"How about some music?" Pete Talbot said, opening his laptop.

Minutes later, furniture had been moved to clear a space for dancing. Lois Lieberman kicked off her shoes and led the way. Paolo leapt to his feet and joined her.

Others joined in, too—Ravi Kapoor and Charlotte Cadell, Pete Talbot and Laura Brenner, Mitchell Fender and the department secretary, Ruth Benjamin.

Edwina sat with Nedda Cake, sipping Port and enjoying the spectacle.

"How did you know there was a child?" Edwina asked her mentor.

Nedda turned to face Edwina, her pale eyes gleaming.

"I didn't. I wanted to help you think outside the box so you could get to the solution. I didn't think anyone had tested the equation for a child, and it seemed worth considering."

Edwina regarded the old woman tenderly. The two sat contentedly, nestled comfortably on a velvet-covered sofa, enveloped in the plush surroundings of Theodore Sanborn's beautiful library. Edwina began slowly to dance, without moving from the sofa, gently moving her shoulders, arms, and head along with the music.

Nedda watched Edwina with amusement, and after a few moments, followed her lead.

*

By early December there were two feet of snow on the ground in New Guilford.

Seth and Sheila Dubin went their separate ways, and not long after, Sheila moved to New York. Seth Dubin and Lois Lieberman began seeing a good deal of each other, now out in the open. Ravi Kapoor and Charlotte Cadell began dating, an eventuality some department members had predicted. Paolo and Francesca Rossetti had a healthy baby boy.

During the first full moon of the snowy winter season Edwina and Will went cross-country skiing on a

cold, starry night.   The hills were illuminated by a
bright, frosty moon, and glittered beneath a black sky
brilliant with constellations.   The only sound besides
the hooting of owls was the quiet shushing of their skis
as they made tracks through the powdery snow.

ABOUT THE AUTHOR

 Elissa D. Grodin is a children's author and novelist. She lives in New York City and Connecticut with her husband, actor/commentator/activist Charles Grodin. They have a son, Nicholas.

Made in the USA
San Bernardino, CA
05 September 2013